Mark Twain

The Man and His Adventures

Mark Twain

The Man  His Adventures

by Richard B. Lyttle

ATHENEUM 1994 • *New York*
Maxwell Macmillan Canada • *Toronto*
Maxwell Macmillan International • *New York Oxford Singapore Sydney*

Unless otherwise noted, the photos in this book were provided through the courtesy of the Mark Twain Project, the Bancroft Library, University of California, Berkeley. Aphorisms used at the start of each chapter were among those written by Mark Twain to open chapters in either *The Tragedy of Pudd'nhead Wilson* or *Following the Equator.*
Quotations from Mark Twain's letters from 1853 through 1868 were taken from Volumes I and II of *Mark Twain's Letters* published by the University of California Press. Quotations from other Mark Twain letters were taken from those collected and first published by Albert Bigelow Paine in his various volumes listed in the bibliography.
Other attributions will be found in the notes at the end of the book.

Atheneum
Macmillan Publishing Company
866 Third Avenue
New York, NY 10022

Maxwell Macmillan Canada, Inc.
1200 Eglinton Avenue East
Suite 200
Don Mills, Ontario M3C 3N1

Macmillan Publishing Company is part of the
Maxwell Communication Group of Companies.

First edition

Printed in the United States of America

10 9 8 7 6 5 4 3 2 1

The text of this book is set in 12/15 Plantin.

Library of Congress Cataloging-in-Publication Data
Lyttle, Richard B.
    Mark Twain : The man and his adventures / Richard B. Lyttle.
        p.   cm.
    Includes bibliographical references and index.
    ISBN 0-689-31712-3
    1. Twain, Mark, 1835–1910—Biography—Juvenile literature. 2. Authors, American—19th century—Biography—Juvenile literature. [1. Twain, Mark, 1835–1910. 2. Authors, American.]   I. Title.
PS1331.L98   1994
818'409—dc20   93-11247

SUMMARY: A biography of one of America's most famous and respected authors, Mark Twain.

This book is for Jean.

❦ ACKNOWLEDGMENTS

As work on this book progressed, it gathered friends. Susan Sasso and Frederic Graeser lent books by and about Mark Twain. John Sheehan and Richard Kirschman sent valuable material. Many others simply wanted to talk about Mark Twain and encourage my efforts. All were helpful.

For research support, I relied heavily on the Mark Twain Project at the Bancroft Library in Berkeley, California, where a team of scholars works diligently to sort, organize, and publish a wealth of original Twain letters and documents.

Michael B. Frank, one of the Project's associate editors, answered my questions and patiently read the manuscript to correct factual errors. His help was invaluable. Sunny Gottberg, Simon Hernandez, and Courtney Clark of the Project staff collected most of the photos and were eager to help in many other ways.

At Atheneum, Senior Editor Marcia Marshall, who has skillfully guided me through many books, again helped bring this one into being with good sense and good cheer.

Jean Lyttle, as encouraging as ever, read and corrected the manuscript and made many sound suggestions.

To all my sincere thanks.

❦ CONTENTS

1

Little Sam

Consider well the proportion of things. It is better to be a young June bug than an old bird of paradise.

On November 30, 1835, in the small village of Florida, Missouri, Samuel Langhorne Clemens, the sixth child of John and Jane Clemens, was born two months before his time.

"I could see no promise in him," his mother recalled. "But I felt it my duty to do the best I could. To raise him if I could."[1]

Although they had four other children, Sam's parents had already lost one boy in infancy and it really seemed that this tiny creature would soon die as well.

Little Sam, as he was called, cried feebly, but the waning Halley's comet in the evening sky gave Jane Clemens hope. She believed comets promised fame and good fortune. At the time the family needed something to keep hopes alive.

Florida was a poor village on roughly cleared land between the north and south forks of the Salt River. Its two unpaved streets, lined with cabins and sheds, were surrounded by fields and the stumps of oak, hickory, and maple trees.

Thirty miles east flowed the great Mississippi. To the west lay the prairie, then known as the frontier.

Florida had been settled four years before Sam's birth in the hope that Salt River, on whose banks virgin cottonwoods and willows still grew, would be cleared and dredged so that barges could carry farm produce of the region down to the Mississippi. With this ambition, the village founders built a wooden church, Florida's largest building, which served as a school during the week and sheltered pigs under its wooden floor year-round.

John Quarles, Little Sam's jovial uncle, had a nearby farm and also owned the store that doubled as an unofficial community center for Florida's four hundred inhabitants.

Most people lived in log cabins, and although the Clemens house had rare clapboard siding, inside it was just as primitive and crowded as the others. In addition to Little Sam, two sisters, two brothers, the parents, and a slave girl all lived in the confines of two small rooms and a lean-to kitchen.

Land was cheap and slaves did most of the heavy work and the daily chores, but the markets for farm produce were far away, and prices were unpredictable. Poverty and an uncertain future, however, could not dampen an optimistic spirit that was voiced everywhere.

The Louisiana Purchase of 1803 had opened an uncharted frontier of seemingly unlimited promise to the people and given America a new destiny.

The future was indeed bright in 1823 when John Marshall Clemens, a young lawyer from Virginia, married one of Kentucky's most delightful daughters. Jane Lampton loved music, laughter, and stimulating conversation. She and her sister would ride miles to attend a dance or a family gathering.

Jane Lampton Clemens, Sam's mother, held the love and respect of her children all her life.

Extremely popular, she had just broken an informal engagement to one eligible young man when she met and agreed to marry Clemens. Thus two opposite natures were joined in a marriage held together more by respect and loyalty than by love. While she was cheerful, he was dour. While she laughed readily, he saw little humor in anything. While she loved company, he preferred solitude and silence.

Being among the first to settle in Jamestown, Tennessee, the couple made a good start. John Clemens, always respected for his sincerity, helped establish the courthouse and began serving as circuit clerk for the Fentress County Court. He built the town's biggest, most costly home, the only home with plaster on the walls and a glass window for every room. With a large house and three slaves, they were clearly Jamestown's most prosperous couple.

Here, in 1825, their first child was born. Because stars and comets fascinated Jane, they named the boy Orion after the constellation.

Soon after Orion's birth, John Clemens made a long-term investment, paying five hundred dollars for a seventy-five thousand-acre tract of forest land some twenty miles south of Jamestown. In the years that followed, the Tennessee land would produce much worry, some promise, and no profit.

Clemens was a better dreamer than businessman. Traveling with the circuit court proved more strenuous than he imagined. He resigned to practice law. He had few clients and decided to become a storekeeper. He moved his family out of their big house into a smaller building that had a front room where he could serve the customers.

A poor merchant, he traded his goods for chestnuts, rosin, lampblack, and other country products that then had to be hauled to Louisville to be converted to cash.

Jamestown did not grow as expected, and in 1831 John Clemens moved his family—which now included two more children, Pamela Ann and Margaret—some nine miles west to Three Forks of Wolf. He built a log cabin that served as home, country store, and post office, but his fortunes continued to decline.

Meanwhile, Jane Clemens's sister, Martha Ann (called Patsy), who had married John A. Quarles, wrote cheerful letters about a promising new town in Missouri. Their farm and store in Florida were already doing well, and the town had a future. Early in 1835 Quarles suggested that the Clemenses come to Florida, Missouri, and form a partnership to run the store. Immediately, John and Jane began packing. The journey over rutted wagon tracks and by riverboats took several weeks.

The Quarleses' invitation may have been largely charity. In recalling his childhood, Sam described his Aunt Patsy and Uncle John as the kindest, most generous people he ever knew. They were certainly a positive influence on his character, and they improved John Clemens's prospects substantially.

Soon after Sam's birth, John Clemens moved his family from the clapboard house to a new, larger home. Little Sam's survival surprised everyone. Although not robust and often sick, he was allowed to play outside soon after he learned to walk. Either his brother Benjamin, born in 1832, or a slave kept an eye on him. By 1838 when Henry, the last of the Clemens children, was born, Sam was part of Florida's herd of barefoot youngsters.

Black and white children explored the fields together. Along the forks of the creek they picked berries and gathered nuts. Sometimes they came home with armloads of flowers.

John Clemens was usually too busy running the store or working on an invention to pay much attention or show affection to his children. Once he spent several months in seclusion trying to make a perpetual motion machine. Jane, with the help now of two slaves, ran the house and cared for the family. The slaves had a powerful influence on Sam. Jennie, who was sometimes beaten because of her rebellious nature, and Uncle Ned, who was famous for his ghost stories, were both devoted to the children. The children, however, were taught early on that a disobedient slave was a serious sinner and a runaway slave was in league with the devil.

The Quarles farm, just four miles from town, became a haven for Jane Clemens and her children. It and the cheerful Quarles family became part of Sam's happiest memories of childhood. He recalled his aunt and uncle's home, warm and practical, as the scene of jolly gatherings. Two log cabins, one divided into bedrooms and the other housing the kitchen, had been connected by a covered veranda where the family gathered for generous meals.

Here Sam could sample turkey, roast pig, chicken, squirrel, duck, goose, venison, rabbit, partridge, pheasant, or prairie chicken. Hot breads steaming from the oven, greens straight from the garden, and heaps of fruit and berries made every meal a colorful, delicious event.

John Quarles, a good mimic and excellent storyteller, loved to play jokes on his young visitors and keep them laughing. Patsy Quarles, a generous hostess, gave Jane much-needed companionship.

Sam and his barefoot gang enjoyed great freedom. They could climb trees in the fruit orchard that surrounded the house, explore the smokehouse that stood against the back fence, or visit the slave quarters that lined the tobacco fields that stretched far beyond the orchard.

And the place had cats. There always seemed to be a new litter, and Sam was among the first to adopt a blind, mewing kitten as his own. He never lost his love for cats.

The dour John Clemens and the cheerful John Quarles could not work together for long. The families remained friendly, but the men soon dissolved their partnership, and John Clemens opened a store of his own across the street from Quarles's store. While young Orion served the customers, the father returned to law, got himself elected justice of the peace, and became known ever after as "Judge" Clemens.

Honest, sincere, and responsible, he also became president of the navigation company that was to dredge the Salt River and bring Mississippi barges to Florida.

But nothing prospered. The town could not support a second store. John Clemens earned little from the law. And the federal money needed to dredge the Salt was never appropriated. Facing poverty, the family also had to deal with tragedy.

On August 17, 1839, Margaret Clemens, age nine, died of what was then diagnosed as bilious fever. Sam, not quite four at the time, remembered little of the event. Soon after, John Clemens moved his family to Hannibal, Missouri. The town stood on the west bank of the mighty Mississippi.

The town and the river worked into Sam's life and character so thoroughly that they became primary elements in the making of a man the world would call Mark Twain.

The town's cluster of white, wood-frame buildings lay in a half circle of hills. Holliday's Hill dominated to the north. The cliffs of Lover's Leap stood to the south. Bear Creek, with many swimming holes, ran down to the river, but it was the big river itself, a mile wide at Hannibal, that fascinated Sam. Steamers, puffing clouds of smoke, churned up and downriver regularly. They looked like floating palaces, bright with lights and gay with music. Smaller boats carried local farm produce or fishermen. Boats stopped often at Hannibal to load or unload cargo and passengers. Some cargo went to St. Louis just a hundred miles south, but there were other shipments bound all the way to New Orleans to be transferred to other boats that could sail to any port in the wide, wide world.

Like other hopeful citizens, John Clemens believed that Hannibal would one day become a major river port. He moved his family into the Pavey Hotel on Hill Street, opened a store on Main Street, and took in what legal business he could find.

Orion, now fifteen, began as clerk in the store, but when the venture failed to prosper, his father sent him to work as a printer's apprentice for the *Hannibal Journal*. Orion felt humiliated. In the society of that day, going from merchant to tradesman represented a huge loss in status. Just the same, the boy learned the printing trade rapidly. Meanwhile, Pamela and Benjamin went to school while Sam and Henry remained at home.

Sam was still frail, and Jane often left him at the Quarles farm where he clearly benefited from the healthy surroundings, robust meals, and the generous spirit of his relatives.

On the farm, Sam usually found himself under the care of Mary, a slave girl. Only six years his senior, Mary was more a playmate than an overseer. The two spent hours exploring the big farm. In a creek not far from the main house they found inviting wading pools. Beyond the creek were big trees that John Quarles had rigged with swings. The woods and fields teemed with birds and wild animals.

There was so much to do. Mornings and evenings, they helped bring in the cows for milking. Then they could ride horses or perch high in an ox-drawn farm wagon. They could climb into an apple tree and sit on a branch eating fruit. They could rove through the meadows picking blackberries. They could help harvest corn or melons. Even though warned not to eat green watermelons, Sam, of course, had to do it. He suffered terrible stomach cramps.

The children visited the slave quarters daily. In one cabin, Sam was fascinated with a bedridden woman who, according to the other slaves, knew how to keep the witches away.

Leaving Sam with the Quarleses relieved Jane Clemens of a major worry. At home Sam rebelled against all rules. He shirked his small chores. He ran off to the river when he was supposed to stay at home looking after Henry. Even at night his habit of sleepwalking worried and frightened the family. Time and again, the other children would wake to find Sam out of bed, shivering in some corner of the house, deep in some troubling dream.

Drownings were common, and Sam was forbidden to swim in the river, but this only made the river more attractive to him. It is hard to say how many times he was pulled, sputtering and coughing, out of the treacherous current. Jane later said that Sam was probably never in real danger because children born to hang are always safe in the water.

At night, Sam, with a mop of sandy curls that seemed too large for his frail body, would sit up in bed and recount the day's adventures for the other children. He spoke slowly, his blue grey eyes quick to see how his listeners waited for his next word. He was lively and full of attention-getting tricks. He had an impish smile. His curls embarrassed him so much he often plastered his hair down with water.

It was typical of John Clemens that he once arrived at the Quarles farm alone when everyone had been expecting him to bring Sam with him to join Jane and the other children. A relative hurried back to Hannibal to recover the forgotten boy.

When he was about five, probably soon after one of his escapes from the river, Sam was put in Mrs. Horr's school. The log building on Main Street housed pupils from age five on up and included some teenage boys and girls. Instruction ranged from the ABCs to long division and included some geography and history and a great deal of reading, grammar, and spelling. Each day began with a Bible story.

Young Sam could not sit still and had taxed the teacher's patience before the first day ended. She sent him outside to fetch a stick and then beat him with it. For Sam the humiliation ruined school forever. Just the same, he learned to read, usually won spelling contests, and eventually graduated to Mr. Cross's school for older children held in a frame house on the town square.

When at the Quarles farm, Sam also went to the country school. Of the two, he liked the country school better because it was not as strict, but in general he regarded all school, including Sunday school, as an unfair infringement on his liberty.

Although elected justice of the peace again in Hannibal, John Clemens still did not prosper. He was forced to sell Jennie and hire Sandy, a slave boy, by the month to help with the housework. Sandy annoyed Sam by singing constantly as he did his chores. When Sam complained, Jane surprised him with a flood of tears.

When she explained that Sandy had just been sold away from his family, that his mother and father were far off in Maryland, and that he had to sing to hide his sorrow, Sam began to wonder about slavery. Although Jane herself said slavery was ordained by God, and everyone in Hannibal believed in slavery, Sandy's story gave Sam his first doubts.

John Clemens unwisely borrowed money to buy a house on the corner of Hill and Main streets. He planned to rent it and build another house on the property for his family, but when his tenants did not pay regularly, Judge Clemens could not pay his own bills. Fortunately, a wealthy cousin in St. Louis came to the rescue. Meanwhile, as in past periods of financial trouble, John Clemens talked of the great potential of the Tennessee land.

He tried to sell it, and when that failed he clerked briefly at the town docks. He quit in anger after his employer criticized his work.

Tragedy again struck on May 12, 1842, when Benjamin Clemens, age nine, died of fever. Sam remembered it well. For years he could see Benjamin laid out in a shroud surrounded by the grieving family, and somehow he managed to blame himself for his brother's death. This would become Sam's typical reaction to family tragedy, repeated with relentless remorse.

The Expanding World

There are those who scoff at the schoolboy, calling him
frivolous and shallow. Yet it was the schoolboy who
said "Faith is believing what you know ain't so."

Soon after Benjamin's death, fortunes seemed to turn at last. Jane began to take in borders. Orion, now seventeen and a good printer, found work in St. Louis and sent home money regularly. Judge Clemens took on some legal cases. Clemens bought a piano for Pamela and ordered construction of the new home at Hill and Main streets.

Shortly after the house was finished, when Sam was ten, the town had a measles epidemic. Many children fell ill and some died. Sam envied the attention the sick received, and when Will Bowen, his best friend, was stricken, Sam sneaked into the sickroom in order to catch the disease himself. He succeeded too well.

Sam lay near death for days, receiving all the attention he yearned for from his grieving family. His recovery surprised everyone, including the family doctor, who, as a last resort, had placed bags of hot ashes on the boy's chest, wrists, and ankles.

Sam recovered to a new period of adventure with more freedom and wider horizons. He and his friends explored the town and its surroundings. They soon knew the citizens and the town scandals as thoroughly as most adults, and were early exposed to violence.

After a gunfight on Main Street, Sam saw the wounded man carried home by friends and laid on his bed. Sam watched as the man struggled for breath beneath the weight of a heavy Bible that had been placed on his chest.

Sam also saw a man stabbed during a drunken argument, and another man attacked by his two nephews. One nephew held the uncle while the other put a pistol to the man's head and pulled the trigger. The gun failed to fire.

When an angry father chased a girl down Hill Street, threatening to lash her with a heavy rope, the frightened girl took refuge at the Clemens house. Jane Clemens stood at the door with her arms spread, defying the man until he dropped his rope and went away.

Sam saw a slave struck dead by his master for a small offense, and he attended the slave auctions at the town dock. Later he described the faces of slaves being sold to southern plantation owners as the saddest he had ever seen. Once an abolitionist was saved from public lynching only after a preacher declared the man crazy and better pitied than punished.

After ditching school one day, Sam decided to hide that evening in his father's office and perhaps avoid punishment. The shades were drawn, but after his eyes adjusted to the dark, Sam saw a body on the office floor. Sam did not know that the victim of a family feud had been brought to the office to die. Terrified, Sam dove out the office window, taking the window sash with him. He was convinced that the body was put there to punish him for missing school.

When a tramp set fire to the jail and died horribly in the flames, Sam could not forget that earlier in the day, he had given the poor man some matches.

But there were many carefree days as well. Jane Clemens often took her family on picnics and steamboat excursions. Once Sam stowed away on a steamer, but a crewman discovered him soon after the boat sailed. Put ashore at the next downriver port, Sam had to wait for his father to come fetch him and punish him.

After he finally learned to swim in Bear Creek, Sam had even greater liberty. He and his friends roamed the river in "borrowed" skiffs. They spent the day fishing, gathering turtle eggs, or playing pirates on Glasscock's (now Tom Sawyer's) Island.

Such boyish pranks and carefree play, remembered years later, would give *The Adventures of Tom Sawyer* a spirit of fun that appealed to readers everywhere. Mark Twain would also rely on the events and characters of his youth for *Adventures of Huckleberry Finn* and many other tales. Most of the fictional characters in these books are portraits of real people.

Sam's friend John Briggs served as the model for Tom Sawyer's friend Ben Rogers. Sid, the goody-goody boy of the tale, was modeled on Henry Clemens, whose good behavior and faithful school attendance used to shame Sam. Tom Sawyer was partly Sam himself and partly his friend Will Bowen, who also was the model for Joe Harper.

Like Tom, Sam wanted to be in charge, and usually organized play and set the rules for the day. Like Tom, it was Sam who got himself elected pirate captain or Indian chief.

Sam wanted respect and attention. He discovered that his slow talk kept people listening, curious to know what he might

Tom Sawyer stands at the center of his gang in this E. W. Kemble illustration from the 1884 edition of Adventures of Huckleberry Finn.

say next. When away from home, he would use swear words to get attention. He often said funny and inventive things, hoping they would be repeated. He also found that a good prank set people talking about him. Like Tom, Sam actually did persuade his friends to whitewash a fence for him.

He tried to act older than his years, and when a girl taunted him for not being able to chew tobacco, Sam had to try it. His retching and shame are clearly described in *The Adventures of Tom Sawyer.*

Sam and his gang spent hours exploring the limestone caves three miles south of Hannibal, caves that provided the scene for the dramatic climax in *Tom Sawyer*. Indian Joe of the book was based on one of Hannibal's destitute characters who actually did hide out in the cave.

The buried treasure of the book was based on a legend of pioneer days that told of French trappers forced to bury their gold when attacked by Indians on the Missouri shore.

Huckleberry Finn, perhaps the most famous character of American fiction, was modeled on Tom Blankenship, youngest son of the town drunkard. This Tom did not have to go to school or to church. No one made him comb his hair or wear starched collars. He could fish or hunt any day of the year. He was a free spirit, adored by other boys and dreaded by adults who saw him as a bad influence.

Although their independence made them more mature than the other boys, Blankenship and Sam had the same spirit of fun. In one day the two boys sold an old coonskin several times to a Hannibal merchant by recovering it again and again through the merchant's storeroom window. When they were finally caught at this game, the whole town, including the merchant, laughed at the trick.

Benson (Bence) Blankenship, Tom's older brother, provided the inspiration for *Adventures of Huckleberry Finn*. Although it was then a crime, Bence sheltered a runaway slave who had taken refuge across the river in a swamp on the Illinois shore. Bence might have collected a fifty-dollar reward for turning the man in. Instead, out of humanity, he took food to the fugitive and kept him alive until a posse got on his trail. The hunters chased the slave into the swamp where he drowned. To their terror, Sam and his pals discovered the body several days later when it rose out of the water in front of their skiff.

At Mr. Cross's school, young Sam began to take an interest in girls. One of his favorites was Laura Hawkins, who became the model for Becky Thatcher. He never ceased trying to get attention from the girls, either in the classroom or on the trees or swings in the school playground.

In class he could usually earn praise by winning the Friday spelling bees. He always wore the school spelling medal proudly. Sam might have liked school if it had offered more freedom, but a lone teacher with a roomful of spirited children had to exert authority with a strict discipline that offended Sam's rebellious spirit.

His chief ambition was to work on the river, possibly as a pilot. Most of his friends shared this dream. In fact, Will Bowen and his two brothers all became river pilots.

Then, Judge Clemens endorsed a loan for a friend who defaulted. All Clemens's property was taken over by the lender. Clemens saved Pamela's piano and a few pieces of furniture, and the St. Louis cousin bought back the Hill Street property, but the family had to rent it and move into a boardinghouse.

Sam's father decided to run for clerk of the surrogate court. The salary would help him recover, and as one of the town's most respected citizens, his election was certain. But he ruined his health in a hard campaign. A freezing rain drenched him on the way home from the swearing-in ceremony and he went to bed with pneumonia.

The doctor visited daily but could do little. Orion returned home from St. Louis. As the patient grew weaker, he spoke again and again of the immense profit still to be realized from the Tennessee land. It sounded like delirium.

On March 24, 1847, just a few hours after talking once again of the land, John Marshall Clemens, age forty-eight, died.

Sam, just eleven, again blamed himself, recalling his disobedience and lack of respect to his father. Jane Clemens viewed the body with the crying boy and made Sam promise never to break his mother's heart again. Sam reverted to a week of sleep-walking.

Faced with another family financial crisis, Orion returned to his printing job in St. Louis. He earned ten dollars a week and sent three dollars of it home. Pamela earned a few more dollars giving piano lessons. Sam and Henry were able to stay in school.

Years later, Sam remembered going to work right after his father's death, but the record shows otherwise. Actually, there was no great change. The family continued to visit the Quarles farm until 1850 when Patsy Quarles died after giving birth to her tenth child. Jane Clemens, who had warned against more children, blamed John Quarles for the tragedy and would not take her family to the farm again.

By then, Sam had gone to work.

3

The Printer

The holy passion of Friendship is of so sweet and steady and loyal and enduring a nature that it will last through a whole lifetime, if not asked to lend money.

Early in 1848 the 12-year-old Sam Clemens became printer's apprentice to Joseph Ament, owner of the *Hannibal Courier*. The boy, full of zeal and energy, quickly mastered the fundamentals of the trade, but he contributed nothing to the family income. Ament provided room and board and some clothing, nothing more.

At the end of each day, Sam slept on a pallet thrown down on the print shop floor. Ament had promised two suits each year, but Sam got just one suit plus Ament's cast-off clothing, which had to be shared with Wales McCormick, the other apprentice.

The old clothes were too big for Sam and too small for Wales. This ill-clad pair at first ate in the Ament kitchen with his slaves, but the apprentices were later allowed to join Pet McMurry, the journeyman printer, in the family dining room. The food was good but too meager for growing boys.

At night, after the family had retired, Sam and Wales often stole apples, onions, and potatoes from the cellar. Sam later remembered that potatoes cooked secretly in the newspaper office could be mouth-watering delicacies.

Those were the days when all print was set by hand. Each letter and punctuation mark was a separate casting that had to be taken from a storage case and composed into lines and columns of type. At the end of a job, the column had to be broken up and the type redistributed to its appropriate bin in the case. A printer's work was judged by his speed and accuracy in setting a column of type. Sam soon had a reputation for setting a clean column.

Wales McCormick remembered Sam as a small, sandy-haired boy, usually with a cigar or pipe in his mouth, who perched at his case on a high stool. When not smoking, Sam invariably sang or hummed. His hands were quick. He seemed tireless.

After a year Sam had such a solid reputation that the jobs demanding the most care and responsibility usually went to him. He could set type almost as fast as McMurry. The boy could also run the press and handle circulation, but Sam liked most to escape from the office and pick up the world news that came in at Hannibal's recently established telegraph office.

He developed a strong sense of responsibility and importance, believing that the town relied on him for its news. The Mexican War was in its final stages at this time, and news was important. Sam rushed from the telegraph office to the *Courier* to set the latest war dispatches in type.

Although he sometimes wrote short articles to fill out a col-

Samuel Langhorne Clemens, age fourteen

umn of type, he had no ambitions to be a writer. He had resolved to be a journeyman printer. With that trade, he could travel anywhere, he could see the world, and he would always find work.

The lure of performing sometimes diverted him. While the circus was in town, Sam yearned to be one of the clowns. When the minstrels came, he aspired to sing and travel with such a show. Once he let himself be hypnotized before a Hannibal audience and reveled in the attention. He told friends afterward that he had only pretended to be under the hypnotist's spell, but no one believed him.

Sam set type so quickly that he could usually leave the shop by midafternoon. He visited friends and enjoyed parties and games. His quick wit, musical talent, and friendly nature made him popular everywhere. Although he had many friends, he usually took Laura Hawkins to the parties, and when Bear Creek froze over, he took her skating.

Both Laura and Sam's brother Henry, who were avid readers, urged him to read more than just the material he set in print. He resisted the suggestion until a lucky accident changed his habits.

By his account, he was walking in the street one windy day when the loose page of a book caught his eye. He picked it up and found that it told a small part of the life of Joan of Arc, the French saint and martyr. He had known nothing about her before, but now he became fascinated with her heroic story.

After reading everything he could find on Joan, he began reading other history books. Sam's self-education had begun. A hunger for learning, which school had never given him, now became so strong it could never be satisfied. His daily reading became a habit that would continue the rest of his life.

He began studying German after persuading a shoemaker to give him lessons and his study of the language continued as a lifelong struggle. He also tried Latin, but gave it up as too difficult.

Sam was still an apprentice at the *Courier* when Orion Clemens returned to Hannibal to start a new career. Because

Orion changed his mind daily, no one could predict what he would do. At first he talked of studying the law. Later, after deciding to be a minister, he organized a temperance rally and gave such a rousing sermon that Sam himself was tempted to become a minister. Sam joked that the safety of the job had attracted him because ministers seemed least likely to be damned.

Orion eventually decided to be a publisher after he found he could buy the *Hannibal Journal* for five hundred dollars. The paper, rival of Ament's *Courier*, already had outstanding debts and Orion had to borrow the money to buy it, but he went to work with great energy. He persuaded Sam to leave Ament, and Henry to leave school to join the *Journal* staff.

Orion expected his brothers to work with his own unlimited zeal. Now, instead of getting his afternoons free, Sam often worked far into the night. As soon as he finished one job, Orion gave him another. And there was no regular pay.

Believing the family welfare depended on the success of the paper, Sam rarely complained. And at first, under Orion's guidance, the paper did succeed.

Although ten years older than Sam, Orion was in many ways less mature. He was a dreamer, never satisfied, never able to settle for long on one occupation, but he was sincere and intelligent and had Sam's gift for meeting people and making friends.

Orion raised the quality of the *Journal* above anyone's expectations. Its editorials set a standard for excellence Hannibal had never seen before. Unfortunately, Orion worked too hard. He tired and fell ill, then lost enthusiasm. The paper gradually lost the ground it had gained.

Orion made matters worse by raising the paper's price. Advertising dropped. In desperation, Orion went to Tennessee to try raising money on the land. He left Sam in charge.

Sam restored reader interest at once with lively, witty news columns. The town, probably tired of Orion's serious tone, was delighted with the paper's new spirit. The *Journal* became the talk of Hannibal when, as a hoax, Sam published an account of a rival editor who tried to drown himself over a failed love affair. Extra copies of the paper had to be printed that day to meet the demand.

Although the story was intended as a joke, Sam based it on gossip that proved to be very close to the truth. The editor, who actually was desperately in love, left town soon after Sam's story appeared.

Orion was outraged on his return and printed an apology for his assistant's irresponsible journalism. It was years before Orion realized his mistake. The *Journal,* he later said, would have shut down all other papers if Sam had been given a free hand.

Meanwhile, in the blush of authorship, Sam sent humorous stories to the Boston *Carpet-Bag* and the Philadelphia *American Courier.* The yarns were printed. And that gave him confidence. Just the same, many years would pass before he would think of himself as a real author.

About this time, Sam, for some reason, wanted Orion to give him a handgun in lieu of his promised salary. Orion refused. He not only opposed guns and violence, he also had no money.

Jane Clemens had been forced once again to take in boarders and Pamela had to resume giving piano lessons. When it seemed fortunes could not sink lower, they did. A stray cow wandered into the print shop one night, upset type, and chewed two expensive ink rollers. Then a fire destroyed most of the equipment the cow had missed. Orion moved the shop into the front room of the Clemens home and somehow kept the *Journal* going for two more money-losing years.

Sam in a more formal pose in 1851 or 1852

Before the end, Pamela left to marry William A. Moffett, a promising merchant from St. Louis, and Sam finally quit. He left Hannibal in June 1853. A month later Orion sold the paper for exactly what he had paid for it.

While Sam went to St. Louis to work as a printer, Orion

took the family to Muscatine, Iowa, and purchased the *Muscatine Journal.*

Although Sam had not told his mother, he intended to stay in St. Louis only long enough to earn his fare to New York. An international exposition had recently opened there in the much-acclaimed Crystal Palace, and Sam yearned to see it.

His adventure soon began. Although it took several days, he was able to travel by rail most of the way from St. Louis to New York. Sam saw himself as a pioneer of the new age of travel, and he arrived in New York proud to report that he had three dollars in his pocket and a ten-dollar bill sewn in the lining of his coat.

Sam's letters to Pamela and his mother reflect the awe and enthusiasm of a country boy on his first venture away from home. He promptly went to the fairgrounds near the present intersection of Forty-second Street and Sixth Avenue, and apparently became so fascinated with a caged "wild man," that he did not get to the Crystal Palace before it closed for the night.

After he did visit the building, he wrote Pamela:

From the gallery (second floor) you have a glorious sight—the flags of the different countries represented, the lofty dome, glittering jewelry, gaudy tapestry, &c., with the busy crowd passing to and fro—tis a perfect fairy palace—beautiful beyond description. . . . The visitors to the Palace average 6,000 daily—double the population of Hannibal. The price of admission being 50 cents, they take in about $3,000.

He undoubtedly made several visits to the Crystal Palace, but the city had many other attractions. In one letter he marveled at the thirty-eight-mile aqueduct that supplied New York with water. He discovered the printer's library where he could spend his evenings surrounded by more than four thousand books.

Sam found a job at John A. Gray's print shop on Cliff Street, and earned four dollars a week. After paying room and board, he had fifty cents left over, enough then to allow a young man to enjoy the big city. He was justly proud of his independence, but the novelty of New York began to fade.

On October 8 he wrote Pamela:

> If my letters do not come often, you need not bother yourself about me; for if you have a brother nearly eighteen years of age, who is not able to take care of himself just a few miles from home, such a brother is not worth one's thoughts: and if I don't manage to take care of *No. 1.*, be assured you will never know it. I am not afraid. . . .

Sam next went to Philadelphia and worked for the *Inquirer* as a substitute typesetter on the night shift. He was paid by the amount of type he set each shift and was fast enough to earn good money. The irregular schedule gave him time to visit art galleries, libraries, and landmarks.

He liked Philadelphia, partly because he was able to earn more there than in New York. He could send a dollar to his mother from time to time. He also became a more serious tourist, largely because his family had given his letters to the papers to be published. Whatever he said about Philadelphia would now get wide attention.

Orion's *Muscatine Journal* printed what was probably Sam's first formal dispatch.

> It is hard to get tired of Philadelphia, for amusements are not scarce. We have what is called a "free-and-easy," at the saloons

on Saturday nights. At a free-and-easy, a chairman is appointed, who calls on any of the assembled company for a song or a recitation, and as there are plenty of singers and spouters, one may laugh himself to fits at a very small expense.

He goes on to describe his visit to a fat lady who was part of a curiosity show: "She is a pretty extensive piece of meat, but not much to brag about; however, I suppose she would bring a fair price in the Cannibal Islands. . . ."

Early in 1854 Sam grew homesick and restless. He visited Washington, D.C., and wrote home from there, describing the tourist attractions. He returned to Philadelphia to work a few more weeks before moving back to New York. He had trouble finding steady work and suffered a loss of confidence. He stayed until summer, but no letters have been found describing his difficulties. Later he said that poverty drove him home.

He rode the train to St. Louis, stayed briefly with his sister Pamela and her husband William Moffett, and then took a steamboat up the Mississippi to Muscatine.

Sam surprised the family at breakfast, causing exactly the sensation he desired. When they rushed to greet him, he feigned anger and warned them to stand back. He held a pistol in his hand. When the shrieks and shouts subsided, Sam laughed with delight and embraced his mother. The gun, something Orion had refused to give him, was a symbol of his manhood and independence. He had earned it on his own.

4

The River Pilot

When angry, count four; when very angry, swear.

Orion wanted Sam to work for him on the *Muscatine Journal,* but Sam declined, saying he could not afford the luxury of working without pay. He did, however, agree to write more dispatches for Orion's paper.

True to his word, Sam began sending dispatches from St. Louis, soon after finding work with the *Evening News.*

In his St. Louis boardinghouse, Sam shared a room with Frank E. Burrough, a chair maker whose enthusiasm for Dickens, Thackeray, Scott, Poe, and other fine authors encouraged Sam to be more selective in his own reading.

While Sam was in St. Louis, Orion married Mary Eleanor Stotts of Keokuk, Iowa. The bride, known to all as Mollie, did not want to leave her hometown, so Orion gave up the Muscatine paper and established a print shop in Keokuk with Henry Clemens as one of his printers. Their mother, Jane

Clemens, came to St. Louis to live with the Moffetts and their two-year-old daughter, Annie.

Sam did not meet Mollie until the next spring, 1855, when he took the steamer to Keokuk. He intended a brief visit, but Orion persuaded him to stay and join Henry in the print shop. Orion promised to pay five dollars a week, but it was the chance to rejoin his brothers that persuaded Sam to stay. It was like the old days. Sam and Henry slept in the printing office and the pay was again irregular. The boys ate with Orion and Mollie.

Fortunately, Sam could live cheaply. Reading had become his main entertainment, and for the evenings, he devised a water pipe with a long tube that made it possible for him to read and smoke safely in bed far into the night.

Sam was not ready for marriage, but he enjoyed female company. A singing class held in a room below the print shop gave him a chance to meet girls and vent his high spirits in music. With a fair voice and a huge collection of songs, he could sit at the piano singing and delighting his listeners for hours.

After speaking at a gathering of printers, Sam was so pleased with the response that he joined a debating club and began developing a polished speaking style. He was soon known in and around Keokuk as a persuasive speaker and a humorist.

Meanwhile, Orion's lack of organization and inability to pay became frustrating for Sam. Time after time, he would be taken from one job to work on another which sometimes meant leaving both jobs unfinished at the end of the day. Orion hoped to satisfy Sam by making him a partner, but this only made Sam feel more responsible for a mess he could not fix.

Secretly, Sam made plans to leave. In the summer of 1856, after reading about the exploration of the Amazon River, Sam decided to go there and make his fortune. He told his mother about his plans and enlisted two friends to join him in the venture, but it was difficult to save money while working for Orion.

Fortunately, Sam found a fifty-dollar bill in the street. After his advertisement brought no one forth to claim the money, he went downriver to visit his mother and the Moffetts in St. Louis.

Although his friends had lost interest, Sam was still determined to go to the Amazon. He devised a plan to finance his travels by writing articles for magazines and newspapers. Back in Keokuk, Sam persuaded the editors of a literary weekly to pay five dollars for each article.

Sam began at once. The first leg of his journey took him to Cincinnati, Ohio, a trip Sam described with rustic humor in a dispatch he signed with the nom de plume of Thomas Jefferson Snodgrass.

It was a start, but Sam needed more money and he was not exactly sure how best to get to the Amazon. He could either head east by rail and sail from New York or go downriver by steamboat and sail from New Orleans. Meanwhile, still in Cincinnati, he took a temporary job setting type and found a place to live.

He met Mr. Macfarlane, a fellow resident of his Cincinnati boardinghouse, who would have a lasting influence on Sam. A self-educated philosopher, Macfarlane was nearly twice Sam's age, but the two became friends at once.

Macfarlane questioned everything, including established political and religious beliefs, and he stimulated Sam to think critically. They talked every night, well into the night, and they loved to discuss the origins of life and speculate on the reasons for creation. Sam questioned what he had been taught about religion and slavery.

He said good-bye to his rare friend on April 15, 1857. As

fate would have it, Sam had decided to descend the Mississippi. He booked passage on the *Paul Jones,* a river packet that carried Horace E. Bixby as pilot.

As soon as Sam entered the pilothouse and began talking to Bixby, the Amazon dream faded, to be replaced by the old ambition for life on the river.

Bixby might not have tolerated a young passenger in his pilothouse, but a sore foot made it painful for him to stand four hours at the wheel. He let Sam steer under his direction. The two men got along well, and it was either during the trip or soon after they docked at New Orleans that Sam persuaded Bixby to take him on as a cub pilot.

Sam would pay five hundred dollars in installments, and Bixby would continue instruction until Sam knew the river well enough to pass the examination for a license. It would take two years, but at the end of that time Sam would have the authority to navigate the twelve hundred miles of waterway between New Orleans and St. Louis.

His training began at once. On his return to St. Louis, Sam borrowed one hundred dollars from his brother-in-law William Moffett to make his first down payment to Bixby. Although he had a quick temper, Bixby treated Sam with kindness and patience. Years later, Bixby recalled that Sam, at twenty-one, was a slender lad with auburn hair, a smooth complexion, and a tendency to "pull" his words in what was more of a hesitation than a drawl.

Like many who had grown up on the river, Sam had an instinct for piloting. He learned quickly, but his greatest asset was his memory. He filled his notebook with descriptions of every snag and shoal, each trick of reflected light, each line of riffles, each eddy of flat water. Once he wrote about it, Sam remembered it.

Though luck was part of the business, you could never count on it, never relax. Even experienced pilots ran boats aground or ripped them open on hidden snags.

Bixby and his cub changed boats often. When the *Paul Jones* went on the dock for repairs in St. Louis, they came back to New Orleans on the *Crescent City*. And so it went. A good pilot never had any trouble finding a berth.

In his zeal to learn, Sam grew to resent the off-hours between shifts when he could not study his river. But in the corporation rooms where pilots met after a journey to trade information and swap yarns, Sam's storytelling talents drew listeners. He was well known on the river long before he became a pilot.

On some layovers in New Orleans, Sam earned a few dollars at night by guarding freight on the docks. He also continued to read and write letters regularly in his spare time. Sam's letters gave his brother Henry an interest in the river trade, and it was through Sam that Henry found his first job as freight clerk.

This led to tragedy. A few months before Sam's training ended, Bixby left the Mississippi to work temporarily on the Missouri River. Sam worked under other pilots. At first Sam sailed on the *John J. Roe,* a happy ship equipped with a dance floor and a piano on the boiler deck where Sam could play and sing in his off-hours.

From the *Roe*, Sam moved to the *Pennsylvania,* where he came under William Brown, who, according to Sam, was an "ignorant, stingy, snarling, fault-finding, mote-magnifying tyrant."[1] Brown made life miserable from the moment the boat sailed from New Orleans on February 6, 1858. The only solace was that Sam's brother Henry, now almost twenty, was on board as third freight clerk. During off-hours, Sam and Henry enjoyed each other's company and befriended Captain John S.

Klinefelter and George Ealer, the other pilot. To the boys' delight, Ealer could quote Shakespeare and play the flute.

But it was not a pleasure trip. When a severe freeze forced Sam to put out in a small boat to search for a safe passage through the ice, he nearly froze. Brown offered no sympathy. Nothing pleased the man. When Sam could not sleep, he says he lay in his bunk plotting ways to kill Brown.

Sam did goad the man. Once, after Sam spun the wheel to head for shore, Brown angrily demanded an explanation.

"I didn't see much else I could steer for," Sam said slowly, "and I was heading for the white heifer on the bank."

In a rage, Brown ordered Sam out of the pilothouse for the rest of the shift.

In *Life on the Mississippi,* published long after he left the river, Sam gives an accurate description of his work as a cub and a pilot. Although he occasionally adopted the experiences of others as his own, he preserved a colorful era in our history that has now vanished. He tells his own story, describing his many friends, the difficulty of learning the river, its risks, the danger of weak boilers, his fight with Brown, and the tragedy that befell the Clemens family.

During the St. Louis layover, while staying with the Moffetts, Sam had a vivid nightmare. He saw Henry dead, laid out in a metal coffin in the front parlor of the Moffett home. A bouquet of white flowers with a single red bloom lay on Henry's chest. Sam was so happy to wake and find Henry alive that he told Pamela about his dream. Neither Sam nor his sister thought of it as an omen.

One day on the downriver run, Brown missed a freight landing and blamed Henry. The pilot claimed that the boy had not called out the landing loud enough. Everyone had heard Henry make the call, but in a confrontation, Brown struck Henry.

Immediately, in a rage of temper, Sam picked up a stool, felled Brown with one blow, and then jumped on the man with both fists flying.

Had he attacked any other man, Sam would never have worked the river again. He might have been arrested. But everyone on board, from Captain Klinefelter down, took Sam's side. When the captain called Sam to his cabin it was not to discipline but to advise him. "Lay for him ashore,"[2] the captain said.

Sam wanted to forget the fight. Not so Brown. In New Orleans, he refused to serve on any boat with Sam again. The captain wanted to fire the pilot and use Sam in his place, but Sam, still unlicensed, volunteered to find another berth.

Thus the ill-fated *Pennsylvania,* with Henry still serving as clerk, set off for St. Louis without Sam. He followed two days later as cub pilot on the *A. T. Lacey.*

News of disaster reached him when the *Lacey* passed close to shore at Greenville, Mississippi. A voice hailed, "The *Pennsylvania* is blown up just below Memphis, at Ship Island! One hundred and fifty lives lost!"

It turned out that half the *Pennsylvania*'s boilers had blown.

Wild with anxiety, Sam hung on every scrap of news as the *Lacey* sped upriver. At first Henry was reported among those who had escaped injury, but later Sam learned that his brother had been scalded beyond hope.

Witnesses said that Henry had actually been blown clear of the blast, apparently uninjured, but instead of swimming to shore, he swam back to the ship to help rescue others. During this heroic effort, steam seared his lungs. Henry lay for several hours on a raft with other survivors before rescuers took him to an emergency hospital in Memphis.

Sam found him there lying senseless on a mattress beside

several other victims. Henry's case was hopeless, but the doctors and volunteer nurses hadn't the heart to tell Sam the truth.

During his long vigil beside Henry, Sam found many ways to blame himself. He had gotten Henry a job on the doomed boat. Sam had been warned in a dream, but he had not warned his brother. Sam had fought with Brown, making it impossible for him to be with Henry when tragedy struck. In his remorse, Sam believed he could have saved his brother.

Volunteer nurses cried for Sam in his grief. They brought him flowers daily. One young doctor, perhaps out of pity, told Sam that Henry might pull through. Clinging to hope, Sam stayed at his brother's bedside night and day.

At one point Henry seemed to rally, but early in the morning on June 21, 1858, eight days after the accident, Henry died in his sleep. It was just three weeks before his twentieth birthday.

Dazed with grief and lack of sleep, Sam let a kind citizen of Memphis show him to a bed. He slept for several days. When he woke, he went immediately to see Henry's body. Most of the dead were being buried in coffins of unpainted wood, but Henry's case had aroused so much interest and sympathy that the citizens had collected sixty dollars to buy something more durable. Sam was stunned to find that his dream had become reality. Henry lay in a metal coffin, and someone had put a cluster of white flowers containing a single red rose on the boy's chest.

Long after Henry had been buried in the Hannibal cemetery beside his father and Benjamin, the tragedy haunted Sam. By some accounts, his hair began to turn gray when Henry died. Sam's eyes, although usually merry and twinkling, sometimes revealed an inner sadness. He still laughed and enjoyed good company, but many who met him at this time could not believe he was just twenty-two. He looked much older.

5

The Pacifist

It is easier to stay out than get out.

On April 9, 1859, after two years of training, Samuel L. Clemens received his license as a Mississippi pilot and went to work at once.

For the first time, Sam began earning a substantial salary and was able not only to finish paying Bixby for his tutoring, but also to send money to his mother, and money plus advice to Orion. Choose a worthy occupation and stick to it, Sam told his older brother.

Sam's audacity can be excused. Already known as a safe pilot, he was being employed at a time when many other, more experienced pilots were out of work. And he was humble on the river, always grateful for his good luck.

One evening, during a stormy upriver trip, he planned to anchor in sheltered water some five miles ahead, but for some reason that he could not remember, he anchored sooner. The next day, in the wake of the storm, he passed the place where he had planned to anchor and found that it had been swept by a gale, with every tree on both banks leveled. His boat would not have survived.

Once, when smoke from a large fire shrouded the river, he ran his boat aground, but it was soon refloated undamaged.

Although such experiences kept him humble, he began to dress like a dandy. He liked suits of blue serge or white duck and was able to afford them. He wore striped shirts and patent leather shoes, and he cultivated a full growth of muttonchop whiskers which made him look more mature.

He still spent much of his spare time reading, writing letters, and even trying to learn French, but he now enjoyed the company of the pilots' corporation rooms more than ever. There, he drew the attention that he loved. He could not only speak with authority about the river, but he also had fresh and intelligent views on literature, history, and politics. But best of all, he told funny stories. Sam's stories were repeated up and down the river. Newspapers printed some of them.

One story, in which Sam brags about his presence of mind in emergencies, was among those preserved in print.

> Boys, I had great presence of mind once. It was at a fire. An old man leaned out a four-story building, calling for help. Everybody in the crowd below looked up, but nobody did anything. The ladders weren't long enough. Nobody had any presence of mind—nobody but me. I came to the rescue. I yelled for a rope. When it came, I threw the old man the end of it. He caught it and I told him to tie it around his waist. He did so, and I pulled him down.

Sam wrote a burlesque of Isaiah Sellers, a stuffy river veteran whose articles in the *New Orleans Picayune* oozed with pompous self-importance. Sellers signed himself "Mark Twain," a nom de plume that stood, in river man's talk, for two fathoms or twelve feet of water, deep enough for any riverboat.

As part of the fun Sam signed himself "Sergeant Fathom." He exaggerated Sellers's style to describe a trip on the river as a series of heroic and fantastic escapes, a kind of odyssey. The story, handwritten for circulation among his friends, touched off storms of laughter. Unfortunately, a friend gave it to a newspaper, and when Sam's tale appeared in print, Sellers was so deeply hurt that he never wrote again.

Sam's remorse lasted long after his friends had forgotten the prank. Years later, in adopting "Mark Twain" as his own pen name, Sam said it was a kind of penitence to Sellers.

There were many happier memories. He and Bixby once treated themselves to a New Orleans banquet that included fish, oysters, mushrooms, and game birds. It cost the lavish sum of ten dollars. He took his mother and two young women as guests on the St. Louis to New Orleans run and shocked Jane Clemens by kissing the girls and dancing the schottische, a "scandalous" dance of the day.

Beyond the river's banks, the shopkeepers, the planters, and the professional people looked down on river men. True, the trade had many tough-minded, rough, hard-drinking men who were inclined to swear and gamble. Just the same, Sam's first rebuff came as a shock. He began calling on a girl he had met when she was a passenger on one of his boats. Things went well until the girl's father discovered he was a river man and abruptly forbade further visits.

Early in 1861 Sam visited Madame Caprell, a New Orleans clairvoyant, who accurately saw his potential as an orator, editor, and writer. Madame Caprell, however, missed the fact that

Sam's career on the river was about to end, that within a few weeks the Civil War would close down all river traffic.

Few predicted the conflict. Like most of his fellow pilots, Sam never dreamed that arguments over slavery and states' rights could bring the great river commerce, their own livelihood, to an end. Even worse, friends suddenly found themselves divided. Bixby declared for the Union. Sam sided with the Confederacy. But he hated taking sides, and as for war, he opposed it.

Wanting time with his family to straighten out his thoughts, Sam rode upriver as a passenger aboard the *Nevada*. The boat squeaked through just ahead of a Confederate blockade at Memphis and was stopped by gunfire at St. Louis.

Missouri had been admitted to the Union as a slave state, but the state legislature, reflecting a majority sentiment, had voted against secession. Slavery was so important to the state's economy, however, that the Union feared Missouri would join the Confederacy after all. A Union army stood ready to invade.

The situation only further confused Sam. He stayed with his mother and the Moffetts for a few days, and then went to Hannibal to visit old friends. Hannibal sympathized with the Confederacy, and several of Sam's friends were secretly organizing a volunteer militia to resist the Union invasion. Caught up in their enthusiasm, Sam went one evening to a meeting of about a dozen young men at Bear Creek Hill. There they agreed to march into the next county and put themselves under the command of Colonel Ralls, a farmer who lived not far from the town of New London. Ralls would tell them what to do.

The next morning when the ragged troop reached the Ralls farm, they received a lavish breakfast and supplies from the colonel and his generous neighbors. They were given so many mules and horses that they were forced to convert from an infantry to a cavalry troop.

Sam acquired an umbrella, a small valise, a carpetbag, an overcoat, two blankets, a quilt, a frying pan, twenty yards of rope, and a yellow mule. That night, using a stable for headquarters, they camped on the Salt River not far from Sam's birthplace. They posted guard and elected officers. As a second lieutenant, Sam became third in the line of command.

It began to rain. False alarms broke their sleep when a guard fired at some tall weeds waving at the wind and another fired at his own horse, which had begun to wander from camp.

Sam, softened by lush riverboat accommodations, quickly developed a distaste for campaigning. In the morning, he also discovered that he had developed a painful boil where a cavalry officer should not have a boil.

Soon after the cold, grumpy, and now underfed volunteers learned that the district general, who was supposed to lead them, had spent the night in well-fed luxury in a warm farmhouse nearby, they voted to disband. Going back to Ralls's farm they lost their way and asked directions from a farmer's wife who chased them off with a hickory pole. Her husband, they learned, was a colonel in the Union army. Such are the fortunes of war.

The troop took shelter for the night in a hayloft, but they had to evacuate quickly when one of them accidentally set fire to the hay while smoking. Sam jumped out the loft window in a shower of burning straw and sprained his ankle.

Now unable to walk or ride, he said good-bye to the troop and found shelter with a friendly farmer. While his friends went on to New London, most to fight and some to die for the Confederacy, Sam became a pacifist.

Union patrols came to the farm searching for rebels, but the farmer did not betray Sam. When he recovered, Sam made his way safely to Keokuk and the shelter of Orion's home.

Many years later, in "The Private History of a Campaign That Failed," Sam gave a vivid, sometimes humorous, description of his brief career as a soldier. He invented the fatal shooting of a soldier to illustrate war's horror, but otherwise the story sticks close to the truth.

Although he had decided not to fight for either side, Sam still faced a dilemma. The southern Confederates could arrest him as a deserter. The northern Union could force him to enlist with the Union. His solution came from an unsuspected source.

Orion, an abolitionist and strong supporter of Abraham Lincoln's new administration, had been seeking a government post. He was at last named territorial secretary to the governor of Nevada Territory, but he had no money for the trip west. He and Sam, however, soon made an agreement. Sam had money left from piloting. He would serve as Orion's secretary and pay the way for both of them.

As a western territory, Nevada had no slaves and little interest in states' rights or any other political philosophies, an ideal climate for a fledgling pacifist.

After Orion bid Mollie and Jennie, his five-year-old daughter, good-bye, he and Sam went to St. Louis for a last visit with their mother and their sister Pamela and her husband. Then they traveled by boat up the Missouri River to St. Joseph, where Sam paid out $150 each as a deposit for seats on the overland stage. He later paid one hundred dollars more for fare, plus an additional freight charge for the big dictionary that Orion thought essential for his duties as secretary.

The trip west, begun in July 1861, was the start of a great adventure that would take Sam to the mines of Nevada and California, to the news beats of San Francisco, and even to far Hawaii, then known as the Sandwich Islands. By the time the venture ended, Sam had changed from a youth with an uncer-

Orion Clemens (courtesy, the Nevada Historical Society)

tain future to a man determined to make his way in the world as a writer and entertainer.

His experiences, joyfully chronicled in *Roughing It,* not only helped him find himself, but also gave him fame as one of a new breed of western writers. Later, he tried to shed the western label, but for years readers expected boisterous adventures, rustic humor, and a youthful spirit of independence from the genius they had come to know as Mark Twain.

The trip west, a mad dash into the sunset behind a plume of dust, was an escape from exacting work as a river pilot and the frustrations of the Civil War. The stagecoach ran day and night, stopping only for meals or to change the team of sixteen horses or mules. Passengers either slept in their seats or on top of a lumpy heap of luggage. They didn't bathe, shave, or change clothes.

Sam and Orion were too excited to let inconveniences annoy them, and they were fascinated by everything they saw. It all seemed new. And when the stage finally reached Carson City, capital of Nevada Territory, Sam was ready to begin a new adventure.

6

The Miner

*Noise means nothing. Often a hen who has merely laid
an egg cackles as if it had laid an asteroid.*

Orion, faced with setting up a new government, actually adjusted to the West faster than Sam, who thought the war would end quickly and that he would soon be needed again as a Mississippi pilot.

The prospect of easy wealth in the Nevada mines fascinated him. He was also enthusiastic about the clear, crisp air and the inspiring scenery of the high desert. Moreover, he caught the spirit of fun of the American West.

He wrote home often but did not tell his family that Carson City had attracted gamblers, gunmen, and prostitutes in large numbers, or that heavy drinking and gunfights were common entertainments.

Orion and Sam moved into Mrs. Margret Murphy's boardinghouse where most other members of the governor's staff lived. While Orion gave full attention to his duties, Sam became an idler and dressed to fit his station.

His costume included a floppy hat that only half hid his untamed auburn hair, a flannel shirt that he usually wore untucked, trousers that he rarely remembered to stuff into his high boot-tops, and a clay pipe, usually lit. When Sam showed himself on a busy corner, supporting one of Carson City's wooden buildings, people stopped to stare. Sam smiled and started talking.

He usually gathered a crowd, and although his stories were often hard to believe, they circulated in parlors and saloons around town. Some new friends were idlers like himself, but Bob Howland, a fellow boarder at Murphy's, had the mining fever and tried to convince Sam that the pick and shovel were keys to untold wealth.

Howland joined the rush to the Esmeralda District some one hundred miles southeast of Carson City and wrote enthusiastic letters to Sam. Finally Sam went to Aurora, the main Esmeralda settlement, to investigate. He stayed with Howland a few days, and someone gave him some mining stock. Sam, however, remained skeptical, and when he found that he held assessment stock that he had to keep paying on to retain his interest, he declared that his doubts had been justified.

Just the same, when it seemed the war might last longer than expected, Sam decided to try taking advantage of the Nevada boom. He would get rich, not by mining, but by selling timber to the miners, timber that was needed desperately to shore up their many tunnels.

Great forests surrounded Lake Tahoe (then Lake Bigler), and anyone could stake a claim there. Sam hiked to the lake with John Kinney, a young friend from Ohio. They claimed a tract of forest simply by building a cabin on the land. Their improvements were nearly complete when they accidentally set fire to the forest. They took to the lake and watched their timber go up in smoke and flames.

Sam, who loved the lake for its majestic scenery, staked other timber claims, some for his relatives, but he never found a practical way to transport logs from the lake to the mines.

By October of 1861 letters home from Carson City showed that Sam had caught the mining fever. By this time he and Orion owned shares in several mines. Mine shares circulated like money. Sometimes the brothers simply received stock as gifts. The stock was highly speculative, worth nothing one day, maybe hundreds of dollars another. Rumors caused as much fluctuation as facts.

While warning of the risk involved, Sam offered to buy stock for the family. Getting an interest in a mine, he wrote, was relatively easy. Finding money to work the mine was more difficult.

In December 1861 Sam joined the rush to the Humboldt District which lay two hundred miles northeast of Carson City on the other side of the high desert. Sam and three other prospectors bought a wagon, two tired horses, and more gear than they would ever need. Just one of the party, Cornbury S. Tillou, a sixty-year-old blacksmith, had mining experience. Gus Oliver and Billy Clagett were both lawyers, of no more use in the mines than a Mississippi pilot.

They had packed such "necessities" as fourteen decks of cards, a cribbage board, a hymnbook, and a keg of beer, but as soon as the wagon wheels sank into loose sand, they were forced to jettison cargo. When the wagon still proved too heavy for the horses, the men got out and pushed.

They trudged through snow, wind, and chilling cold. The cold kept them awake at night. They could not get lost because tombstones, bleached bones of draft animals, and charred remains of shacks and wagons marked their route. During the entire eleven-day trip, Sam and his friends expected an Indian raid at any time, but they saw no Indians until just outside of Unionville, the major settlement of the new district. Then they faced a band of Piute warriors. By giving them generous measures of flour and sugar, Sam may have averted a fight.

The town, huddled in the bottom of a canyon, consisted of eleven shacks, some no more than lean-tos dug into the hillside. Sam and his friends took over one of these and soon found that stones rolling off the hill could break through the cloth roof and raise havoc with the furnishings. Sam's claim, however, that a cow paid a visit through the roof was probably one of his many exaggerations.

In *Roughing It* Sam occasionally made things seem worse than they actually were, but his disappointment was real. He was so sure when he arrived in Unionville that he would find masses of silver exposed on the earth's surface that he slipped away from his friends to spend a few minutes collecting his personal fortune.

It soon became painfully clear, however, that mining was not to be so easy. Tillou located a promising outcrop of rock, so they staked a claim and began digging a shaft. Hard rock stopped them again and again.

"One week of this satisfied me," Sam wrote. "I resigned."[1]

Speculation suited him better than digging. Reports from other mines sent their stock soaring or plunging according to the nature of the news. A few carefully selected ore samples shown to the right people could inflate the value of stock and make a speculator rich. Such deceptive practices, it seems, had started the Humboldt rush, but Sam was one of the last to give up hope in Humboldt mining stock.

Even when he headed back to Carson City with Tillou, Sam

carried worthless stock certificates with him and talked of returning to the Humboldt District.

Early in 1862 Sam and Tillou nearly drowned trying to cross the Carson River. They had to wait for the flood to subside. Later, they lost their way in a snowstorm. Sam had given up hope when they made camp that night, but by dawn the storm lifted and they found themselves just a few steps from a warm, well-provisioned cabin where their host directed them to Carson City.

Sam, now impatient for more prospecting, stayed in Carson City little more than a month before heading for the Esmeralda District to join Bob Howland. The two friends already owned assessment stock in the Horatio and Derby, one of the district's most promising mines, and Sam wanted to give it his personal attention.

Although it was April, frozen ground delayed work at the Horatio and Derby. However, a fifty-two-foot tunnel, dug the previous season, had tapped a spring. There was enough water coming from the tunnel, Howland said, to run a stamp mill, and stamping mills were needed to crush their ore, the first step in the smelting process. Sam thought there might be enough water to crush ore from other mines in the district. Meanwhile, he used his inventive mind to explore possible improvements in smelting.

His letters home remained optimistic, but after a glowing description of Lake Bigler prompted Pamela to think of coming west, Sam wrote to dissuade her, describing the dry lake beds of Nevada that were covered with sunbaked deposits of alkali salts.

. . . If the Devil were set at liberty and told to confine himself to Nevada Territory, . . . he would come here and loaf sadly around, awhile, and then get homesick and go back to hell again. . . . I have had my whiskers and moustaches so full of alkali dust that you'd have thought I worked in a starch factory and boarded in a flour barrel.

He did not want his family to know about his poverty. He and Howland shared their small, ill-heated cabin with two other men. The roof leaked. Sometimes they went to bed hungry. But they all had pride. More than once, to impress the neighbors, they collected empty fruit cans and champagne bottles to give the trash behind the cabin some class. Those who did not know them might have thought that they lived in luxury.

Orion sustained Sam at this time. It was understood that the brothers would share their mining profits. Sam often put both his and Orion's name on newly acquired stock. The Clemens brothers eventually owned stock in thirty Esmeralda mines with the total face value of five thousand dollars. They both believed they would soon be worth much more—millions!

While waiting for the Horatio and Derby mine to thaw, Sam worked with pick and shovel at the Dashaway, the Live Yankee, the Flyaway, the Annapolitan, and the Monitor.

Meanwhile, newspapers had printed several of Sam's early letters home, and when copies of these papers reached Carson City, Sam gained some modest attention. Orion took immense pride in showing Sam's letters to friends. This led to the reprinting of some of the letters in the *Territorial Enterprise* in Virginia City. Readers agreed that Sam was an entertaining correspondent. Sam was pleased with the reaction, and when editors of the *Enterprise* asked for dispatches from Esmeralda, he agreed at once.

There was no pay, but it gave him something to do, and the dispatches earned attention. Although humorous and often exaggerated to the point of burlesque, his accounts captured the spirit of the western mines. In one letter he described a decrepit horse, probably one of those that had pulled his wagon to the Humboldt District. In another letter he wrote about an egotistical lecturer who had entertained the men at Esmeralda. A full report of the speech by "Professor Personal Pronoun," as Sam called him, was not possible because the type cases did not have enough *I*'s.

Sam and his friends could not afford Aurora's gambling halls and saloons, but there were more modest entertainments. Sam distinguished himself at a dance one evening by doing at least one turn with every partner available and by dancing every known step, perhaps even inventing some new ones.

Spring brought renewed hope and activity to the district. Investors or their agents came from all parts of the world to stimulate speculation and inflate the value of everything. The price of flour hit one dollar a pound.

Caught up in the madness, Sam bought more stock, but he realized by now that mining eventually came down to hard work and experience. "The pick and shovel are the only claims I have any confidence in now," he wrote.

In this spirit Sam took a ten-dollar-a-week job at an ore-crushing stamp mill to gain practical experience, but illness forced him to quit after the first week. He said the quicksilver and other chemicals used at the mill had made him sick.

He recovered in time to join a friend in a futile search for the legendary "Cement Mine," where nuggets, reportedly, could be plucked from a cement formation like fruit from a tree. The venture, which Sam later called a vacation, took him to the shores of Mono Lake, which he described vividly in *Roughing It.*

Chapter 7

The Reporter

Truth is the most valuable thing we have. Let us economize it.

Sam's transition from miner to newspaperman was not as abrupt as his recollections suggest. Long after he had wearied of disappointment and hard labor with pick and shovel, he continued to believe that his mining investment would one day make him rich.

By July 1862, however, he knew he had to have a steady income. He asked Orion to write the *Sacramento Union* "and tell them I'll write as many letters a week as they want for $10 a week."

Although nothing came of the *Union* proposal, Joe Goodman at the *Territorial Enterprise* heard about it and asked for Sam on his staff. Would Sam work for the *Enterprise* full-time at twenty-five dollars a week?

Sam hesitated. Writing letters from the mines was one thing, but leaving the district to join the staff of a newspaper was something else entirely. It seemed too much like giving up.

In a letter to Orion written August 7, Sam reported the status of their various mining interests and added that he had written the *Enterprise* to ask when he might be needed on the paper. Meanwhile, he intended to take a long walk into the hills.

"I want to know something about that country out yonder."

He hiked alone through some seventy miles of wilderness. He spoke or wrote very little about this experience, but most likely, he simply wanted to be alone, to think about his future. He did get one thing sorted out. On August 15, 1862, soon after returning to Aurora, he wrote Pamela that he did not intend to return to piloting.

"My livelihood must be made in this country." Although he did not mention the *Enterprise* offer, he described with journalistic flair an Aurora cabin he shared with Dan Twing and Dan Twing's dog.

> The mansion is 10 x 12 with a "domestic" roof. Yesterday it rained—the first shower for five months. "Domestic," it appears to me, is not water-proof. We went outside to keep from getting wet. . . . The dog is not a good hunter, and he isn't worth shucks to watch—but he scratches up the dirt floor of the cabin, and catches flies, and makes himself generally useful in the way of washing dishes. . . ."

In the fall of 1862, Sam walked 130 miles from Aurora to Virginia City to begin work on the *Enterprise*. He startled the staff with his ghostly appearance. White alkali dust covered his slouch hat, shoulder-length hair, faded shirt, and untucked trousers. He carried a blanket roll over one shoulder and wore a navy revolver on his hip. A sore right leg made him list like a sinking ship.

William Wright, already an admirer of Sam's letters, welcomed Sam warmly, showed the apparition around the paper's office, and took him to his boardinghouse where he found a room for him. Wright, who wrote under the nom de plume of "Dan De Quille," introduced Sam to the new job and community.

Virginia City, twelve miles northwest of Carson City, was booming with the development of the famous Comstock Lode when Sam arrived. To get the silver, miners had turned nearby Mount Davidson into an anthill of tunnels. Some of the miners had even burrowed under the streets and buildings of Virginia City and neighboring Gold Hill.

Despite its boomtown atmosphere, Virginia City rivaled San Francisco for sophistication. The people dressed up, and Sam exchanged his miner's duds for a fancy outfit that included polished boots, a starched shirt, and a long, broadcloth coat. Sam's transition from dirt miner to writer, humorist, and lecturer thus began in a haberdashery shop. He was twenty-six years old and eager to master a new trade.

Sam found an excellent teacher in Joe Goodman. Ever since he acquired control of the paper in 1861, Goodman insisted that his reporters go to the source for stories. The *Enterprise* would not print rumors. It soon gained a reputation for reliability throughout Nevada and California. Just before Sam arrived, the paper had moved into a new building on C Street with new presses and a staff of expert typesetters.

Reporters had great freedom to gather the facts and give their views. They never ran out of subject matter. Virginia City teemed with adventurers, gamblers, successful businessmen, hordes of hopeful miners, entertainers, politicians, prostitutes, gunmen, mountain men, celebrities, tourists from many lands, and yes, newspaper reporters. When news was slow, members of the *Enterprise* staff interviewed each other.

The spirit of fun and optimism that filled the town suited

Sam's character and his mood perfectly. Always curious, he reveled in the variety of characters who surrounded him. Sam's cordial nature, puckish humor, and slow drawl won attention everywhere, and readers soon learned to recognize his work in the paper. He could be clever, unpredictable, and extremely funny or serious and even profound.

Sam quickly grew confident enough to begin playing jokes both on his fellow workers and his readers. Newspaper hoaxes were common and usually harmless, or at least well intended. Sam invented one of his best to deflate the stuffed-shirt coroner of the Humboldt District.

During a spasm of self-importance, when the coroner began withholding information from reporters, Sam "discovered" a prehistoric skeleton and invented a detailed account of the coronor's inquest into the cause of "death." It made the official appear foolish.

Sam wanted readers to see the story as a hoax, and reported that the deceased was found in a sitting posture with one thumb to his nose. Most people missed the meaning of the gesture, however. His story was reprinted as the truth by other papers throughout North America. It caused a sensation. The coroner, who could not answer all the requests for more information, was outraged, but Sam kept the hoax alive for several days by sending news clips to several colleges. Soon scientists joined those demanding to know more about the discovery.

It was common in the days of slow communication for papers to reprint stories from other towns, and after several California papers had criticized Nevada's wild mining speculation, Sam, with Goodman's approval, wrote about a man who went crazy after losing all his money in a California water stock fraud. In Sam's account of the "Empire City Massacre," only the water stock fraud was real. The "city" was no more than a crossroads, and the berserk man who killed his wife and seven of his nine children before cutting his own throat from ear to ear did not exist.

Sam's graphic story, however, was reprinted widely. Even other Nevada papers, whose editors should have known better, ran the story as top news. When the hoax was admitted, the outrage was so heated that Sam offered to resign, but as Goodman predicted, the uproar was soon forgotten.

Sam himself, to the delight of others on the staff, could be easily fooled. Steve Gillis, one of the compositors, frequently hid Sam's pipe or his candle simply to watch him fuss and swear as he searched for these necessities. Sam made a sign forbidding anyone to touch his candle, but the next time he turned his back, both candle and sign would have vanished. Sam raged while his friends laughed.

Joe Goodman enjoyed Sam's company and was among the first to appreciate his deeper nature. The two dined together frequently, and Goodman discovered that Sam could recite verse after verse of poetry and seemed to grasp many fine points of philosophy.

During one of their dinners Sam persuaded Goodman to let him report meetings of the territorial legislature, which was about to convene in Carson City early in 1863. Sam lacked political experience, but Goodman guessed that this might make his reports even more entertaining. Indeed, Sam did use his innocence to his advantage by writing about the politicians and their manipulations as if they were newly discovered phenomena.

The politicians themselves liked this fresh approach and for the most part were willing to excuse a few mistakes. Several were even helpful, but Sam's greatest support in his early days at the capital came from his rival, Clement T. Rice, the reporter for the *Virginia City Union*. Although they made fun of each other in their columns, they worked in harmony in covering the legislature. Sam called Rice "the Unreliable," but in truth, he was a careful reporter as well as a friend and teacher.

Orion, now with his wife and daughter, lived in a comfortable Carson City home where Sam could stay while covering the legislature. Orion and Mollie entertained often, and Sam's well-informed opinions, delivered with wit, helped make the parties successful.

Because James W. Nye, the territorial governor, was frequently absent, Orion served often as unofficial acting governor, a position that gave Sam an advantage in his competition for news stories. He also had friends in the legislature itself. Billy Clagett, the lawyer who was his mining companion in the Humboldt venture, now represented that district. Jack Simmons, speaker of the house, became one of Sam's closest political friends.

Sam's unsigned reports were easily recognized by readers, but he wanted to put a name on them. He discarded several possibilities, until he learned that Captain Isaiah Sellers had recently died. Mark Twain sounded just right for a pilot-turned-reporter, and Sellers would have no further use for the name. Goodman approved and "Mark Twain" appeared for the first time on a Carson City dispatch published on February 3, 1863.

No one, least of all Sam, realized how famous the name would become. He did not even mention the new byline in his letters home. In fact, he belittled his success as a newspaper reporter. On February 16, 1863, he told his family, "They pay me six dollars a day, and I make 50 per cent. profit by only doing three dollars' worth of work."

He continued to describe the mining stock that would one day make them all rich, and he acquired more stock. Mine owners often gave reporters free stock, hoping to exchange it for favorable reports on their mines. Although Sam referred to it as "blackmail," it's unlikely that he turned it down. Unfortunately, Sam had the habit of holding on to his stock long after its value had evaporated.

When the legislature adjourned in the spring of 1863, Sam returned to Virginia City with a high opinion of himself, and because Sacramento and San Francisco papers had reprinted Mark Twain's reports regularly, his pride was not entirely unjustified.

Nevada stock speculation rose to new heights in the boom that year. So did crime. Writing home one April evening, Sam interrupted his letter saying, "I have just heard five pistol shots down street—as such things are in my line, I will go and see about it." He resumed a few hours later. "The pistol did its work well—one man—a Jackson County Missourian, shot two of my friends, (police officers,) through the heart—both died within three minutes. . . ."

Despite such dramas, Sam had grown restless. He and Clement Rice, the rival reporter and friend, decided on a vacation in San Francisco, and on May 3, 1863, this notice appeared in the *Enterprise*:

Mark Twain has abdicated the local column of the ENTERPRISE, where, by the grace of Cheek, he so long reigned Monarch of Mining Items, Detailer of Events, Prince of Platitudes, Chief of Biographers, Expounder of Unwritten Law, Puffer of Wildcat, Profaner of Divinity, Detractor of Merit, Flatterer of Power, Recorder of Stage Arrivals, Pack Trains, Hay Wagons, and Things in General. . . . He has gone to display his ugly person and disgusting manners and wildcat on Montgomery street [San Francisco]. In all of which he will be assisted by his protegee, the Unreliable.[1]

They intended to stay in San Francisco one month, but Sam did not go back to Carson City until July. He apparently financed this extended vacation through the sale of mining stock, but he also wrote for the *San Francisco Morning Call*. He had enough money to send some to his mother.

On June 1 he wrote,

> The Unreliable & myself are still here, & still enjoying our-selves. I suppose I know at least a thousand people here—a great many of them citizens of San Francisco, but the majority belonging in Washoe [the Comstock District]—& when I go down Montgomery Street, shaking hands with Tom, Dick & Harry, it is just like being in the main street of Hannibal & meeting the old familiar faces. I *do hate* to go back to Washoe. . . ."

In the same letter he described trips he and Rice made to Oakland and San Leandro and north to Benecia, the former state capital of California. He explored San Francisco thoroughly and sailed on the bay in a friend's yacht. Sam figured that before returning to Nevada, he would know the city better than most of its citizens.

He was indeed reluctant to return. In a later letter he told his family that returning to Nevada would be like returning to prison.

When he finally did return to Virginia City he had a close call with death. He was sound asleep in his boardinghouse when a fire, perhaps set by an arsonist, began raging. Sam jumped to safety from his window, but the building and most of his possessions, including stock he said was worth three hundred thousand dollars, were destroyed.

✧ CHAPTER **8**

Breaking Away

*It were not best that we should all think alike; it is
difference of opinion that makes horse races.*

Sam returned to work with confidence and in his usual spirit of
fun wrote his mother that no paper could pay him what he was
worth and that he might make his job on the *Enterprise* pay
twenty thousand dollars a year if he weren't so lazy.

> But I don't suppose I shall ever be any account. I lead an easy
> life, though, & I don't care a cent whether school keeps or
> not. Everybody knows me, & I fare like a prince wherever I
> go, be it on this side of the mountains [the Sierra Nevada] or
> the other. And I am proud to say I am the most conceited ass
> in the Territory.

He went on to describe his political influence. "Oh, I tell
you a reporter in the Legislature can swing more votes than any
member of the body. . . ."

Rice did his best to deflate his rival's ego. Once when Sam took time off to cure one of his colds at a nearby hot springs, Rice, who agreed to fill in for him, made up an apology.

The piece, printed in the *Enterprise* over Mark Twain's name, asked forgiveness from all the "victims" Sam had written about, including politicians and his rival reporters on the *Union*.

Replying in his paper the following day, Sam withdrew the apology and called Rice "a reptile endowed with no more intellect, no more cultivation, no more Christian principle than animates and adorns the sportive jackass-rabbit of the Sierras. . . ."[1]

In September 1863 Sam took another San Francisco vacation. Although his stay was brief, it included nights at the theater, fancy balls, and countless games of billiards with friends. He came back to work in time to cover the First Annual Fair of the Washoe Agricultural, Mining, and Mechanical Society. As society secretary, Sam received three hundred dollars a year.

A constitutional convention followed the fair, and Sam spent several hectic days reporting debates over the form Nevada's government should take. He became so popular among the delegates that when the meeting ended he was elected to head the "Third House" of the Nevada legislature. This mock organization, with many complex rules of conduct, had been created by the politicians to ridicule the two actual legislative bodies of government.

Sam returned to Virginia City in time to greet Charles F. Browne. Sam and Browne, known to the world as humorist and lecturer Artemus Ward, became friends at once. Browne intended to give just one or two talks in Virginia City before moving on, but found such a warm welcome and such congenial company among the *Enterprise* staff that he stayed about two weeks. He predicted a great future for Mark Twain, and apparently took some pains to make his prediction come true.

He urged Sam to keep polishing his style and sharpening his wit, and stressed his need to branch out and travel. Sam must start writing for other publications, Browne said, and later recommended Sam to some New York editors.

In addition to giving practical advice, Browne also set an example for all his admirers on the art of enjoying life. At the banquet following his final lecture in Virginia City, Browne raised his glass in solemn toast:

"I give you Upper Canada."

After everyone sipped his wine politely, Goodman asked, "Of course, Artemus, it's all right, but why did you give us Upper Canada?"

"Because I don't want it myself," the wit replied.[2]

The evening could only grow sillier after that. And when midnight struck and the company was reminded that it was now Christmas Day, the party turned into a revel.

At dawn, Mark Twain and Artemus Ward stood on a rooftop watching the sunrise. A sober policeman, thinking the two celebrities were burglars, might have shot them if Goodman had not intervened.

The farewell banquet was such a huge success that Browne was easily persuaded to extend his stay. Before New Year's Day, 1864, however, he had resumed his travels. Sam and Browne never met again.

Thanks to Browne, Sam became more serious about his writing. He soon sent the *New York Sunday Mercury* an article; it was accepted.

Although Sam now wanted to move to San Francisco, his duties kept him in Washoe. When the Territorial Legislature reconvened on January 12, 1864, he once again moved in with Orion and Mollie to report proceedings.

As he had boasted to his mother, Sam's endorsement of a

An 1864 photo shows Sam between his friends William H. Clagett and A. J. Simmons of the Nevada legislature. The caption reads: "Three of the suspected men still in confinement at Aurora."

bill, along with the backing of Simmons and Clagett, could indeed influence the legislature, but he was never accused of abusing this power. Despite his lighthearted spirit and his ready wit, he knew when to be serious. He kept his promises, did nothing in secret, and remained scrupulously honest in all his dealings with the lawmakers.

"Sam's word was as fixed as fate," Orion said.

To show their respect and appreciation, his many friends on the legislature called a meeting of the "Third House" late in

January. The charity affair raised two hundred dollars needed to complete a church. Sam's speech, making witty fun of the politicians, was not written down, but it reportedly kept everyone howling. At the end, Sam received a gold watch inscribed "Governor Mark Twain." Even Rice "the Unreliable" called the evening a success.

Sam had grown comfortable with his pseudonym. Although his family and his old friends would continue to call him Sam, the politicians, his fellow reporters, and most of his new friends called him Mark. He began signing some of his letters with his new name.

With spirits as high as they had ever been, death again humbled him. Eight-year-old Jennie Clemens, Mollie and Orion's only child, and Sam's loving niece, died of meningitis on February 1, 1864. The blow devastated her parents and Sam.

Grief may have made Sam emotionally vulnerable. When the famous actress Adah Isaacs Menken came to Virginia City to play the title role in *Mazeppa,* a popular romance of the day, Sam, along with all the other men in town, became infatuated. He wrote her a long letter. Miss Menken pretended to be offended but soon allowed him to call on her. By then, however, Sam had apparently recovered his senses.

Although the Civil War was being fought far away, residents of the territory were reminded regularly of the bloody tragedy by appeals for funds to treat the wounded. These Sanitary Funds as they were called financed most of the care in Union hospitals, and raising money for the funds had become competitions between states, cities, and territories. Volunteers organized charity dances, banquets, fairs, and other events to benefit the funds.

Although Sam did not invent the famous flour sack auction, his ardor in promoting it led to embarrassment and trouble. Goodman had gone on vacation, leaving Sam in charge of the

An engraving depicts the famous "Sanitary Sack" carried by Reuel Colt Gridley.

Enterprise when the fifty-pound sack of flour began making news. Originally, it had been carried a mile and a half by a man who lost an election bet. To get rid of it at the end of the walk, the man offered to auction it, with proceeds going to the Sanitary Fund.

Bidding was so strong, and the auction raised so much in money and pledges, that the sack was taken to another town for another auction. And so it went from town to town, with each town trying to outbid the other in total money raised.

Newspapers gave this story a great deal of space and attention, and on May 17 Sam and several other citizens formed a procession led by a brass band to circulate in and around Virginia City with the sack of flour. They held auctions in Gold Hill, Silver City, Dayton, and Carson City before returning to Virginia City for the final auction. They had already raised some ten thousand dollars in the other towns, and citizens of Virginia City were determined to do better.

And they did. In an hour and a half of frenzied bidding, the auction raised some thirteen thousand dollars. Sam, who represented the *Enterprise* in the bidding, would not be topped by the *Union* representative, and made sure the sale had closed before leaving to write his report. After he left, however, the *Union* man slipped in a late bid, well above Sam's.

A silly battle of words began in both papers. Sam charged the *Union* of reneging on what it had pledged. The *Union* called Mark Twain "a vulgar liar." Before anyone could come to their senses, Sam challenged the *Union* owner James L. Laird to a duel, and Laird accepted.

Sam was stunned. Like most other citizens of the territory, he often wore a six-shooter on his hip, but he never had needed to defend himself with it, so never really learned to use it. Now, there seemed no way to avoid a fight.

Steve Gillis, who feared for his friend's life, fortunately acted as his second and resolved the dispute in a typically Gillis fashion.

After a sleepless night, Sam, with Gillis and others, went early to the dueling grounds for pistol practice. They propped a wooden post against a barn door and Sam pretended it was Laird and tried to hit it. After missing the post several times,

Sam recalled that he aimed for the barn to see if he could hit that.

To make matters worse, Sam and his friends heard Laird practicing nearby.

> Now just at this moment a little bird, no bigger than a sparrow, flew along by and lit on a sagebrush about thirty yards away. Steve [Gillis] whipped out his revolver and shot its head off. Oh, he was a marksman—much better than I was. We ran down to pick up the bird and just then, sure enough, Mr. Laird and his people came over the ridge and they joined us. And when Laird's second saw that bird with its head shot off he lost color, he faded, and you could see that he was interested.
>
> He said: "Who did that?"
>
> Before I could answer, Steve spoke up and said quite calmly, and in a matter-of-fact way, "Clemens did it."
>
> The second said, "Why, that is wonderful! How far off was that bird?"
>
> Steve said, "Oh, not far—about thirty yards."
>
> The second said, "Well, that is astounding shooting. How often can he do that?"
>
> Steve said languidly, "Oh, about four times out of five."[3]

Soon after this conversation, both sides agreed to cancel the duel.

Meanwhile, his zeal for the Sanitary Fund had embroiled Sam in a heated dispute with the ladies of Carson City whom he had insulted. After an evening of drinking, Sam had amused William Wright by concocting a hoax story charging that the ladies had misappropriated proceeds from their charity ball. Unfortunately, Sam and Wright left the office without destroying the story. A printer, following standard procedure, saw it on Sam's desk and set it in type. A shocked Sam read the story in the paper the next day.

He apologized profusely and tried to explain, but nothing he could say calmed the storm. The *Union*, of course, did all it could to keep the controversy alive.

Coming on top of his near duel with Laird, the business soured Sam on Nevada Territory. There was just one thing left to do. On May 29, 1864, Sam and Steve Gillis boarded the stage for San Francisco.

Sam later claimed that he and Gillis had to leave because they had broken the law against dueling, but he was impatient for a change of scene. He also had a plan to make money.

He intended to go to New York and make a killing selling Nevada mining stock, but the steamer he planned to catch sailed just a few hours before he and Gillis reached San Francisco. This was the first in a series of setbacks.

His mining stock suddenly lost value, so instead of living in luxury as he had planned, he and Gillis had to go to work for the *San Francisco Morning Call.* Steve set type and Sam worked as a reporter. To his dismay, Mark Twain, well known to Nevada readers, did not command much attention in San Francisco. He was reduced to routine work, checking the police court in the morning, drifting about for whatever he could find in the afternoon, and ending the day at the theaters where he caught a few minutes of whatever performances were being offered. He recalled it as "fearful drudgery—soulless drudgery—and almost destitute of interest. It was an awful slavery for a lazy man . . ."[4]

They lived in one cheap rooming house after another. Evening entertainment consisted of a late meal, a few beers, and a game or two of billiards before retiring to their room.

Sam usually smoked and read in bed by candlelight for an hour or so before going to sleep.

The Chinese in San Francisco were cruelly persecuted, and to his shame Sam once took part in this persecution. It happened when he and Gillis shared a room that overlooked the shacks of a Chinese quarter. By lofting beer bottles onto the tin roofs of the shacks, he and Gillis could watch the reaction from behind their curtains.

Later Sam's better character prevailed when he stood up for the Chinese. One day he saw some butchers set their dogs on a Chinese person while policemen stood by doing nothing. Sam wrote a story attacking the police, but the *Call* would not print it.

Some days later when he came upon a policeman asleep on duty, Sam stood over the man, fanning him with a cabbage leaf until a large crowd gathered. Sam knew that it was pointless to try to get anything printed against the police, but the cabbage leaf story was repeated by word of mouth all over the city.

Life became more lively for Sam as he began to collect new friends. Frank Soulé, a fellow reporter on the *Call,* wrote poetry that Sam admired. Bret Harte was secretary at the United States Mint and soon to become editor of the *Californian.* He encouraged Sam to write for it and for the *Golden Era.*

The *Californian* paid twelve dollars for each article, the *Golden Era* only five dollars, but as a leading literary magazine, the *Era* attracted young writers who gave Sam the companionship, stimulation, and encouragement he needed.

Harte soon put Sam on the staff of the *Californian.* Sam's articles became more polished and his humor more refined than ever before. And thanks to the magazine articles, his reputation as a humorous writer began to spread throughout California.

The *Morning Call* printed Sam's report that a man who had gone up in a rocket had forced evacuation of a large region of the city where the projectile was expected to come down. Some readers believed this fantasy and wrote angry letters, protesting the evacuation.

Despite their hard work, Sam and Gillis were still living close to poverty. Sam had to give up some mining stock because he could not keep up payments of the assessments. He also was forced to sell the furniture he had left in Virginia City to cover a bank loan. Tougher times lay ahead.

CHAPTER 9

New Horizons

Prosperity is the best protector of principle.

In October 1864 Sam and the *Call* parted by mutual agreement, and his income fell to the few dollars he earned from his magazine articles. Sam's description of his plight in *Roughing It* apparently exaggerates the truth only slightly.

> For two months my sole occupation was avoiding acquaintances; for during that time I did not earn a penny, or buy an article of any kind, or pay my board. . . . I felt meaner, and lowlier and more despicable than the worms. During all this time I had but one piece of money—a silver ten cent piece— and I held to it and would not spend it on any account, lest the consciousness coming upon me that I was *entirely* penniless, might suggest suicide. . . . I had pawned every thing but the clothes I had on; so I clung to my dime desperately, till it was smooth with handling.[1]

During this time Steve Gillis and Sam apparently got in a saloon brawl. Small and feisty, with a temper, Gillis was quick to start a fight. Sam, with his ready smile and slow drawl, could usually restore peace before fists began flying. This time, however, the dispute left bruises and a great deal of damaged property.

On December 4, 1864, according to Sam's account, he and Steve left San Francisco to escape arrest. Steve returned to Virginia City while Sam went to Jackass Hill in Tuolumne County, California, where Steve's brothers, James and William Gillis, were prospecting for gold.

The brothers, along with partner Richard Stoker, introduced Sam to pocket mining. The method was to follow traces of gold with pan and shovel to its source, sometimes a very rich vein in a rock outcrop. A pocket miner with very little equipment could earn a fortune in a single day, but if there were millionaires in the hills when Sam arrived, he did not find them. He bunked with Stoker in a one-room cabin just as humble as those he lived in while mining in Nevada.

James Gillis owned another claim near Angels Camp in Calaveras County, and on January 22 Sam and Jim left Jackass Hill to work the holding. When heavy rains kept them under cover for days on end, the miners of Angels Camp entertained each other with stories. Sam, with plenty of good stories to tell, may have suggested this recreation. In any case, it changed his life.

During one of these storytelling sessions, one miner called Ben Coon told a story about a jumping frog contest. Sam wrote the story down as soon as he could and then began reworking it. He was still mulling it over when he returned to Jackass Hill.

"When Sam came back," William Gillis recalled, "he went to work on the Jumping Frog story, staying in the cabin while we went out to work our claims and writing with a pencil. He used to say: 'If I can write that story the way Ben Coon told it, that frog will jump around the world.'"[2]

Sam returned to San Francisco on February 26, 1865. The threat of arrest had evidently passed, but he remained desperately poor until Joe Goodman of the *Territorial Enterprise* offered him twenty-five dollars a week for daily dispatches from San Francisco. This allowed him to begin clearing his debt and give full attention to his writing. Meanwhile, Steve Gillis returned from Nevada to once again share room and board with Sam.

Although his *Enterprise* letters kept him busy, he finished the frog story and sent it to Artemus Ward who helped find an editor who agreed to publish it. Sam also sold articles and sketches to several California publications, and because some of his past work was being reprinted as well in magazines and papers across the nation, his reputation grew modestly.

The September 1865 issue of the New York *Round Table* carried a report on western humorists and said in part, "The foremost among the merry gentlemen of the California press, as far as we have been able to judge, is one who signs himself 'Mark Twain.' Of his real name we are ignorant. . . ."[3]

In New York the *Saturday Press* published "Jim Smiley and His Jumping Frog" on November 18, 1865. Within days, thanks to hundreds of reprintings, readers across the country were laughing over Mark Twain's story. Now his reputation soared.

Mollie and Orion were forced to return to Keokuk in the fall of 1866. His job in Carson City had been eliminated when Nevada became a state. He intended to practice law, and Keokuk promised more clients than Nevada.

Meanwhile, Sam looked west. On January 13 the steamer *Ajax* sailed from San Francisco on its maiden voyage to the

Sandwich Islands and revived Sam's itch for travel. Actually, he had been invited to join the dignitaries on that first trip, but commitments to Goodman and other editors kept him in San Francisco.

On March 7 when the ship sailed again, Sam was indeed aboard, a traveling correspondent for the *Sacramento Union*. He carried letters of introduction to scores of islanders, including many government officials and members of Hawaii's royal family.

The trip took eleven days, and when the ship docked in Honolulu, Sam at once fell under the romantic spell of a tropical Eden. He had not been prepared for the beauty of the islands or the charm of the people. Everything surprised him, and he wrote with the exclamation of constant discovery and delight. "God, what a contrast with California and the Washoe!"[4]

Each day unfolded like a dream. He could not meet enough people. He had to go everywhere. He extended his stay from one month to four. His readers were charmed. He sent the *Union* twenty-five dispatches, and some were reprinted by other papers on the East and West coasts. The dispatches later provided the basis for the final chapters in *Roughing It*.

Sam did not succumb to the languid tropics and turn lazy. Instead he worked avidly with what at first seemed limitless energy. He toured the island of Oahu on horseback, first inspecting its coastline and then climbing the mountains for breathtaking views. After seeing the scattered bones that marked a battlefield, he researched the history of the island's natives.

Although he carefully described the volcanoes, beaches, and other geological beauties, he knew that the heart of any region could only be found in its people. He focused on them and continued to hold this perspective in his future travel writing.

King Kamehameha V invited Sam to his palace for a banquet and entertainment provided by native dancers and singers. Sam had come to the islands with a background of racial prejudice which gave his early dispatches a patronizing slant. The king and his court, however, were so warm and generous and treated Sam with such respect that his attitude changed to genuine admiration. He realized that white missionaries and Yankee traders had taken cruel advantage of native innocence and generosity.

From Oahu, Sam sailed off to visit the other islands. He stayed in many plantations and many small towns and never missed a natural wonder. On the Big Island of Hawaii, he climbed 13,680 feet above sea level to the top of Mauna Loa and followed a dangerous, faintly marked path across the crusted lava of a volcanic crater.

In June, soon after returning to Oahu, he met Anson Burlingame, who was returning to his post as United States minister to China. Sam, however, had to get out of bed to meet the distinguished visitor. He had at last worn himself out, and he had such painful saddle boils that it was difficult to walk.

Despite his discomfort, Sam impressed Burlingame, who quickly saw Sam as a young man of exceptional genius. He encouraged Sam to take his future more seriously, waste no effort in developing his talent, travel at every opportunity, and pick friends who would stimulate him.

Burlingame had an air of dignity that Sam admired. He was immensely generous, and although he had great political power, he knew how to use it wisely. Their association was brief, but Sam remained grateful for Burlingame's advice and example. He returned to bed after that first meeting, but a startling development brought the two men together again.

On June 15, 1866, fifteen starving seamen had landed on a remote Hawaiian beach in a small boat. They were sole survivors of the clipper ship *Hornet,* which was lost to fire. With a ten-day supply of food and water, the men had lasted forty-three days in an open boat and managed by heroic seamanship to find land.

Sam could make a spectacular news scoop, but when the *Hornet*'s men were brought to an Oahu hospital where they might be interviewed, Sam's boils made it too painful to stand. Burlingame, understanding Sam's plight, had him carried on a cot to the hospital. There Burlingame asked the survivors questions and Sam wrote down their answers. That was the easy part. Sam still had to write his story and there was very little time.

A steamer was to leave for the mainland early next morning, and Sam wrote all night to complete his report. A friend tossed the package containing his manuscript onto the deck of the ship just as it was pulling away from the dock.

While most island newsmen sent off no more than a few paragraphs on the survival, Sam's day-by-day account of the remarkable adventure, complete with interviews, created a sensation and showed that Mark Twain was not just another humorist.

Years later in "My Debut as a Literary Person," Sam credited Burlingame for making the news scoop possible. But even if there had been no story, Burlingame set Sam on the road to fame simply by having faith in the young man. Sam thus entered a new, more ambitious, more ordered phase of his life.

℘ CHAPTER 10

On the Stage

The man with a new idea is a Crank until he succeeds.

Soon after returning to California, Sam went to Sacramento and asked the *Union* publishers to pay him three hundred dollars for the *Hornet* story. To his surprise, they paid that and added more for additional expenses.

Sam then expanded his *Hornet* story and was delighted when *Harper's Magazine* accepted it. At last the "Mark Twain" byline would be printed in a prestigious publication. But later, when "Forty-three Days in an Open Boat," appeared in the magazine, the story was signed "Mark Swain." Sam was devastated.

Meanwhile, he wrote articles for the *New York Weekly Review* and the *Californian*. In September the *Sacramento Union* hired him to cover the California State Agricultural Society's thirteenth annual fair. He gave the stock shows and the horse races most of his attention.

Sam planned a book on the Sandwich Islands, but there was

so much interest in that tropical haven that he wanted to take more immediate advantage of it. Why not a lecture?

Having grown weary of newspaper work, Sam saw lecturing as an escape, a chance to travel, and a better income. His friends encouraged him, and before he could change his mind, he booked a recently completed music hall for the night of October 2, 1866. Then he got cold feet.

Speaking before a gathering of Nevada's "Third House" was not the same as speaking to the paying public. What if people didn't like his talk? Worse yet, what if no one came? But it was too late to pull out. Sam had announcements printed saying in part:

> A splendid orchestra is in town, but has *not* been engaged. . . .
>
> Magnificent fireworks were in contemplation for this occasion, but the idea has been abandoned. . . .
>
> Doors open at 7 o'clock. The trouble begins at 8 o'clock.[1]

Tickets were one dollar in the dress circle and fifty cents in the family circle.

Sam was beside himself with apprehension. He was sure no one would come. He rehearsed his talk again and again, committing it to memory, and weighing every pause, word, and gesture for best effect. Sam had learned from Artemus Ward that how you said something was just as important as what you said. That is, if you had an audience.

He had worried needlessly. On the night of his lecture, every seat was filled and the aisles were crowded with standees. When he walked on to the stage with knees trembling, the house erupted with applause.

Although he had rehearsed thoroughly, Sam's style seemed fresh and informal. His pauses suggested that he was trying to think of a word or phrase. The pauses also gave the audience time for laughter and applause. As in his letters, he took the stance of the innocent observer and found he could make people laugh without resorting to exaggeration or rustic humor.

Although he is remembered as being hilariously funny in his first lecture, Sam also made a serious case for Sandwich Island statehood. Opposition, he knew, was due largely to racism, prejudice against the islands' large population of dark-skinned Polynesians, but by describing the natives with sympathy and understanding, Sam hoped to overcome such nonsense. Ninety-three years would pass, however, before Hawaii won admission as the nation's fiftieth state.

Sam earned four hundred dollars profit from his talk, and it set San Franciscans talking. Although urged to give a repeat performance, he decided instead to take his act on the road. He persuaded Denis McCarthy, a friend from the *Enterprise*, to be his manager and book talks in Sacramento, Marysville, Grass Valley, Nevada City, Red Dog, and You Bet, all in California.

After speaking to packed houses in each of these towns, he went to Nevada and spoke in Carson City, Silver City, Virginia City, Gold Hill, and Dayton. His fears that audiences might remember his Sanitary Fund troubles and be hostile proved unfounded. In fact, his receptions in Nevada were even warmer than in California.

A busy pace of two or three talks each week gave Sam the chance to polish his style. Practice before audiences taught him how to build suspense and get the most out of a joke or colorful phrase. He changed a few words to heighten effect, but because he made no substantial changes, he refused to repeat his talk in the same town. Why let people discover that his informal chat was actually a carefully rehearsed and highly calculated performance?

Steve Gillis, now working in Virginia City, decided to stage a hoax that would give Sam all the material he needed for a second lecture. Gillis enlisted several old friends to "rob" Sam one night on the road from Gold Hill to Virginia City. Sam, they knew, would be carrying the proceeds from his Gold Hill lecture with him. The road was lonely. It would be dark.

Denis McCarthy, the business agent, would be with Sam, but Gillis let McCarthy in on the plot.

The prank went off as planned except that Sam's Gold Hill friends delayed him so long after the lecture that the waiting "robbers" nearly froze. Gillis also miscalculated Sam's reaction. The plain fact is that being robbed at gunpoint is no joke. Though Sam remained outwardly calm as the gunmen took his money and relieved him of his gold watch, he could not easily forget his terror.

Gillis thought it was a great lark. He remembered Sam's response when confronted by masked and armed men. "Don't flourish those pistols so promiscuously. They might go off by accident." And Gillis enjoyed hearing Sam plead in vain to retain the treasured watch given him by the "Third House" of the Nevada legislature.

It still seemed a great joke when Gillis and his friends hurried into Virginia City to wait for their victim to appear in his favorite saloon. There, after Sam told him what had happened, Gillis lent him one hundred dollars. The unsuspecting Sam then bought drinks for everyone.

William Wright, who had not been let in on the plot, interviewed Sam and wrote a story of the robbery that appeared the next day in the *Territorial Enterprise*. Sam offered a reward for the capture of the gang and agreed to give a talk on his experience.

McCarthy booked a lecture hall and began selling tickets, but the day before the talk, a friend revealed the hoax. In a rage, Sam canceled the lecture and threatened to bring charges against Gillis and his gang.

Joe Goodman had to reason with Sam a long time before he changed his mind, but even when his money and his watch were restored, he was still angry when he took the stage back to San Francisco. Gillis was hurt and puzzled. In earlier days, he was sure Sam would have passed the whole thing off with a laugh.

Sam had indeed become more serious. He always spoke fondly of Gillis in the years that followed, but they saw little of each other after the "robbery." Sam retained McCarthy as business agent, but only briefly. Goodman and William Wright, however, remained his close friends.

Before giving in to the demand for another appearance in San Francisco, Sam revised his Sandwich Islands lecture. Meanwhile, he determined to expand his travel experiences and persuaded the publishers of the *Alta California* in San Francisco to sponsor a trip around the world.

The plan was not carried out, but Sam thought he was making a start around the world on December 15, 1866, when he sailed from San Francisco on the steamer *America,* with Captain Ned Wakeman in charge. He would stop in New York to see publishers and visit his family in St. Louis before beginning his circumnavigation.

Much had changed during the five and a half years since he had been on the East Coast. The Civil War, fought to a bloody end, had left a more mature, more realistic nation, a nation with few illusions. Sam himself, now thirty-one, had matured, had tasted fame, and had gained an appetite for more.

Captain Wakeman proved to be one of the most colorful characters Sam had ever met. Although the captain had not spent a day in school, he knew the Bible by heart. His profanity could blister the ears of any ship's stoker and make a deaf man blush. He knew every part of the world. His observations were original, wise, entertaining, and apparently endless. Sam, in his new role as travel writer, took careful notes on conversations with the captain. Later, Wakeman would serve as the model for Captain Ned Blakely in *Roughing It* and for Captain Stormfield in other stories.

Sam's journey home turned into a harrowing saga. After the ship docked at San Juan del Sur in Nicaragua, the passengers crossed the Isthmus of Panama by jungle trail and riverboat. It took two days to reach Greytown on the Caribbean coast. There they boarded the *San Francisco* for New York. Cholera struck soon after the ship sailed. Three victims died. The ship made speed for Key West, but within hours, the engine broke down. Two more died as the ship drifted on rolling swells in the Gulf of Mexico. The ship's doctor ran out of medicine.

Through some oversight, the ship was not quarantined when it finally reached Key West, and twenty-one passengers left the ship at once. Sam stayed on board and sailed for New York. Another two died before the ship docked on January 12, 1867.

In New York Sam's discussions with publishers were at first disappointing. None showed interest in a book on the Sandwich Islands or a collection of his newspaper sketches from Nevada and San Francisco. Even Sam's main hope, a collection of humorous stories including "Jim Smiley and His Jumping Frog," was rejected repeatedly, but Charles Henry Webb finally agreed to bring the book out. Sam was delighted. He had become convinced that he could not draw lecture audiences on the East Coast until he became established as an author.

Meanwhile, he sent dispatches to the *Alta*, describing New York through the innocent eyes of a tourist. He had not seen the city for thirteen years, and much had changed. He walked miles and miles, taking in the sights, jotting down notes.

He met friends from the Far West and Missouri who were now living in New York. Most of them urged him not to wait for a book to be published and to start lecturing at once, but the vision of failure terrified Sam.

He met old friends and developed new ones in newspaper offices. The *Sunday Mercury,* the *Evening Express,* and the *New York Weekly Review* all agreed to buy his travel dispatches. His plans to circle the world on his own changed, however, when he learned of a fascinating opportunity. Through the coming summer, the Reverend Henry Ward Beecher, a popular minister of the Plymouth Church in Brooklyn, had engaged a ship for a tour of the Holy Lands and other Mediterranean regions. The passenger list already included William Tecumseh Sherman, of Civil War fame, and several other notables, including Beecher himself. The ship was a handsome side-wheel steamer, the *Quaker City.*

Sam, with a letter of introduction from a mutual friend, went to Brooklyn to see Beecher on February 3. He may have seen a representative and not Beecher himself on that visit because he went back a few days later with a newspaper friend. This time he went to the ship's booking office.

Unfortunately, Sam and his friend had been drinking, and neither made a favorable impression on Captain Charles C. Duncan, who would command the *Quaker City.* Duncan was understandably skeptical when Sam was introduced to him as a Baptist minister.

"You don't look like a Baptist minister," the captain reportedly observed, "and really, Mr. Clemens, you don't smell like one either."[2]

On March 1 Sam returned, made a better impression, and

put down $125 as a deposit for a ticket to the Holy Lands. He wrote to the *Alta* the next day.

> Prominent Brooklynites are getting up a great European pleasure excursion for the coming summer, which promises a vast amount of enjoyment for a very reasonable outlay. The passenger list is filling up pretty fast.
>
> The steamer to be used will be fitted up comfortably and supplied with a library, musical instruments and a printing press—for a small daily paper to be printed on board. . . . The steamer fare is fixed at $1,250 currency. The vessel will stop every day or two, to let passengers visit places of interest in the interior of various countries, and this will involve an additional expense of about $500 in gold. The voyage will begin the 1st of June and end near the beginning of November—five months—but may be extended by unanimous vote of the passengers. . . . Isn't it a most attractive scheme? . . .[3]

Without waiting for a reply, Sam boarded the train for St. Louis on March 3.

His family welcomed him warmly. His mother, now almost sixty-four, thought Sam looked older, but otherwise unchanged by his fame. He was still full of mischief and high spirits. While in St. Louis, Sam agreed to several public appearances. He told his jumping frog story to a Sunday school class, and later gave his Sandwich Islands talk as a benefit for another Sunday school. He broke a rule by repeating the talk the next day in the same place.

In early April he spoke to full houses in Hannibal, Quincy, and Keokuk. He saw Mollie in Keokuk, but Orion was in Tennessee at the time, seeing once again if something might be realized from the family's land.

When Sam returned to New York in mid-April, an agent for the *Alta* was waiting for him with a check for $1,250, the price of a *Quaker City* ticket. On top of this good news, Charles Henry Webb told him that in May the collection of humorous stories, his first book, would appear in shops and newsstands.

CHAPTER 11

The Innocent

Nothing so needs reforming as other people's habits.

On April 20, 1866, the New York papers listed Mark Twain officially as one of *Quaker City*'s passengers. Reverend Beecher and General Sherman had both withdrawn from the excursion for personal reasons, leaving Sam as the only genuine celebrity.

He did not feel like a celebrity. Thinking that his book would make him well known on the East Coast, he had at last agreed to lecture, but the book's publication had been delayed. As May 6, the date for the lecture, approached, Sam grew frightened. He had booked the Cooper Union, then the largest auditorium in the city. Sam did not see how he could fill it.

His fears seemed justified. The "Imperial Troupe," a famous Japanese juggling act, and a Broadway play starring a popular actress, were both set to open May 6. This was competition enough, but five days before his lecture, Sam learned that Schuyler Colfax, Speaker of the House of Representatives, had

COOPER INSTITUTE

The Sandwich Islands.

By Invitation of a large number of prominent Californians and
Citizens of New York,

MARK TWAIN

WILL DELIVER A

Serio-Humorous Lecture

CONCERNING

KANAKADOM

OR,

THE SANDWICH ISLANDS,

AT

COOPER INSTITUTE,

On Monday Evening, May 6, 1867.

TICKETS FIFTY CENTS.

For Sale at CHICKERING & SONS, 652 Broadway, and at the Principal
Hotels.

Doors open at 7 o'clock. The Wisdom will begin to flow at 8.

To Sam's surprise, his first lecture in the East filled Cooper Union to capacity.

picked that day to talk at a famine relief charity for the Southern states.

Sam ordered more advertisements for his talk and had free tickets sent to every public school teacher in and around New York, but again he had underestimated his popularity.

He could hardly believe the scene when he arrived at the auditorium. Long lines of people stood in the street waiting to get in. Carriages had stopped traffic.

Sam walked onto the stage to a storm of applause. With no empty seat in sight, he launched into his standard Sandwich

Islands lecture in the best of spirits. His enthusiasm was contagious. The audience responded with wave upon wave of laughter and applause.

Reviewers raved about the lecture and a few days later, they began praising his book. It had at last appeared with the jumping frog story and twenty-six other tales. Although it won acclaim, Sam was upset over its many typographical errors, and although he dedicated it to "John Smith" on the theory that every John Smith in the country would buy it, American sales proved sluggish.

"As for the Frog book," he wrote his mother, "I don't believe that will ever pay anything worth a cent. I published it simply to advertise myself & not with the hope of making anything out of it."

Although sales did not exceed five thousand books in America, pirate publishers in England sold forty-three thousand copies. Copyright laws of the time did not protect him, and Sam received nothing from the foreign sales. The experience started him campaigning for laws that would assure royalties for authors from all publications of their work.

The weeks before sailing were crowded for Sam. He lectured to full houses in Brooklyn and again in New York. He arranged to write travel letters for the *Herald* and the *Tribune*, two New York papers with a combined circulation of 255,000. Meanwhile, he fell behind in his letters to the *Alta*, and he was not proud of what he had written so far.

As his day of departure neared, family worries added to Sam's troubles. "My mind is stored full of unworthy conduct toward Orion & toward you all," he wrote his mother and the Moffetts. It was true that Orion and Mollie were desperately poor, but only a remorseful Sam could find ways to blame himself for their troubles.

An engraving printed in Frank Leslie's Illustrated Newspaper *in 1867 shows the* Quaker City *steaming into a storm.*

The *Quaker City,* a vessel of eighteen hundred tons with a top speed of ten knots, had steam-driven side-wheels and auxiliary sails. She left the Brooklyn dock on June 8 with sixty-five passengers. A storm forced them to anchor inside the harbor.

The tourists used the time to get acquainted and sing hymns to the accompaniment of the ship's organ. Sam soon realized that most of his traveling mates were not only older than he by far, but they were also much too reserved to appreciate his high spirits and rustic humor. Luckily, he found a few young travelers and enough others who were young enough in spirit to make the trip fun.

Daniel Slote, his chubby cabin mate, was young and quick to smile. The owner of a stationery company, Slote, according to Sam, was "a splendid, immoral, tobacco-smoking, wine-drinking, godless room-mate who is as good & true & right-minded a man as ever lived—a man whose blameless conduct & example will always be an eloquent sermon to all who shall come within their influence. . . ." Slote had "many shirts, and a History of the Holy Land, a cribbage-board, and three thousand cigars. I will not have to carry any baggage at all."

Although Dr. Abraham Reeves Jackson, a forty-year-old widower, was older, Sam admired his experience, wisdom, wit, and conversational skills. Dr. Jackson, who amused everyone by saying silly things with a straight face, became one of Sam's closest shipboard friends.

Julius Moulton and John A. Van Nostrand, both young and shy, were also regular companions. Among the older crowd, Mary Mason Fairbanks proved to be the most sympathetic and helpful. A veteran traveler, retired teacher, and wife of Abel Fairbanks, co-owner of the *Cleveland Herald,* Mrs. Fairbanks was also sending home travel dispatches for publication. She described the dinner hour:

> There is one table from which there is sure to come a peal of contagious laughter, and all eyes are turned toward "Mark Twain," whose face is perfectly mirth-provoking. Sitting lazily at the table, scarcely genteel in his appearance, there is nevertheless something, I know not what, that interests and attracts. I saw today at dinner, venerable divines and sage looking men, convulsed with laughter at his drolleries and quaint original manners. . . .[1]

Helpful without being overbearing, Mrs. Fairbanks, of all the passengers, had the greatest influence on Sam. He read his *Alta* letters to her before dispatching them and accepted her suggestions with gratitude. Like Burlingame, she urged Sam to treat his talent with more respect, to take himself more seriously. She and Sam remained friends until her death, long after the *Quaker City* adventure ended.

Sam's letters, later revised and edited for *The Innocents Abroad,* did indeed maintain the attitude of innocence that had earlier charmed his fans.

The ship's frequent layovers made possible an overland trip to Paris and an inland excursion of Italy accompanied by Slote and Dr. Jackson. In Italy Sam reported with wide-eyed wonder that he had seen enough relics of the true cross for several simultaneous crucifixions.

In Greece, when a routine quarantine prevented the passengers from landing, Sam and three others secretly hired a boat, went ashore at night, and saw the Parthenon by moonlight. Had they been caught, they might have spent six months in jail. Their daring caused horror and some envy among the more timid passengers.

In the Black Sea, the passengers of the *Quaker City* were invited to visit Alexander II, the czar of Russia, in his summer palace near Odessa. Sam wrote the formal address for the occasion.

While visiting the palace he reported, "I got on very familiar terms with an old gentleman, whom I took to be the head gardener, and walked him about the gardens, slipping my arm into his without invitation, yet without demur on his part, and by and by was confused again when I found out that he was *not* a gardener at all, but the Lord High Admiral of Russia! I almost made up my mind that I would never call on an emperor again."[2]

Usually just a few words in his notebook were all Sam needed to record an experience, but if dates or measurements were important he might fill a page with notes. Occasionally, he drew crude sketches of a building or scene, just enough to revive his memory. He pretended to have fierce artistic pride in his "art."

Although behind schedule at first, Sam soon caught up with his reports. He sent fifty letters to the *Alta*, six to the *New York Tribune*, and two to the *New York Herald*. Each averaged four thousand words, and when put together there was indeed enough to fill a book. His production, considering the distractions and inconveniences of travel, is remarkable. And through it all he maintained the pose of the world's laziest man.

In recalling the voyage, most of Sam's fellow passengers complained that he spent so much time writing that they missed his company.

At the Holy Land, Sam and five other passengers started from Beirut on a long, overland trek that eventually took them to Jerusalem. It was the hottest season of the year. The travelers were exhausted at the end of each day. Sam fell ill in Damascus, possibly with cholera, but he continued. Later, when Slote got sick in a small Syrian village, the others continued on their journey, but Sam stayed behind until Slote was well enough to travel.

One of the *Quaker City*'s youngest passengers, seventeen-year-old Charles Jervis Langdon, son of a wealthy coal dealer in Elmira, New York, did not at first appreciate Sam. As time passed, however, Langdon became an ardent fan. When Langdon showed Sam a picture of one of his two older sisters, Sam was smitten. Olivia Langdon's sweet, delicate face seemed the prettiest thing Sam had ever seen. He asked to borrow the picture. Langdon refused but let Sam come to his cabin often to look at the likeness.

When the *Quaker City* finally turned for home, Sam had grown weary of travel and impatient with many of the passengers. Although he traveled for a week in Spain while the ship lay at Gibraltar, he wrote nothing about his adventures. From Cadiz, he wrote Joe Goodman:

Sam and Charley Langdon posed for this formal shot in 1868.

... this pleasure party of ours is composed of the d——dest, rustiest, ignorant, vulgar, slimy, psalm-singing cattle that could be scraped up in seventeen States. They wanted Holy Land, and they got it. It was a stunner. It is an awful trial to a man's religion to waltz it through the Holy Land.

Resentment against Sam erupted when mail delivered at Gibraltar included papers from home that carried some of his letters. His greatest offense, it seemed, was praising Mrs. Fairbanks's social poise at the czar's palace and lamenting that other ladies on the tour had not conducted themselves as well as she.

This resentment festered as the ship sailed across the Atlantic, and when she docked on November 19, 1867, the party separated without great regret. Mrs. Fairbanks was one of the few among the older passengers to express appreciation of Mark Twain.

> Those who had the good fortune to share with him the adventures with which his remarkable and grotesque narratives have made the public familiar, recall with interest the gradual waking up of this man of genius. His keen eyes discerned the incongruities of character around him, into which his susceptibility to absurdities gave him quick insight.[3]

Sam vented his feelings in his final letter to the *New York Herald* which appeared a few days after the ship's return. He called the trip "a funeral excursion without a corpse," and complained that dancing had to be stopped when some of the older passengers considered it sinful. Their main recreation, he said, was dominoes which "they played until they were rested, and then they blackguarded each other until prayer-time."[4]

Although Sam stayed in touch with a few, including Charles Langdon, Dan Slote, and Mary Fairbanks, he was glad to forget the others. Meanwhile, to his delight, the letters had brought him new fame.

12

Sam in Love

Man will do many things to get himself loved,
he will do all things to get himself envied.

Soon after his return Sam went to Washington, D.C., as private secretary to Senator William M. Stewart of Nevada. The senator, who had known him in Nevada, thought Sam just the man for the job. Sam was eager for work and expected to have spare time enough to continue writing for various papers.

Indeed, the *New York Tribune,* the *New York Herald,* the *Alta,* and the *Enterprise* carried Mark Twain's dispatches from Washington. He soon reported lightheartedly that he was no longer secretary to the senator. Stewart and Sam remained friends, but it became clear to both that they could not work together.

Although Sam did not have the temperament for politics, he did try to use the influence of friends there to get a Washington job for Orion. Sam himself turned down tempting offers from

An engraving made in 1868 shows Sam as he looked as a western correspondent and Holy Land traveler.

the State Department and the post office, but he could find nothing suitable for Orion.

Sam's social success in Washington compensated perhaps for his political failure. He attended countless parties and was often asked to speak or respond to a toast. A member of the Washington Correspondence Club described Sam's response to a toast as "the best after-dinner speech ever made."[1]

Sam still owed money on side trips made during his travels, but he turned down bids to lecture. He now had literary ambitions.

Although sales of the frog book had been disappointing, he wanted to try again, and jumped at the proposal from a subscription publisher for a book on his *Quaker City* venture. The American Publishing Company in Hartford, Connecticut, like most large publishers of the day, sold its books in advance of publication. The method helped avoid losses. With advance or subscription sales, publishers knew exactly how many volumes to print.

Sam began exchanging letters with Elisha Bliss, Jr., who ran the American Publishing Company. Meanwhile, he went to New York at the end of 1867 for the Christmas holidays, spending one boisterous evening with his former shipboard companions Dan Slote, Jack Van Nostrand, and Charley Langdon. Later, Langdon took Sam to dinner with his family at the St. Nicholas Hotel. Although some records say that Sam met Olivia Louise Langdon on December 23, 1867, it is clear that he was still in Washington on that date. The two probably met for the first time soon after Christmas in the dining room of the hotel where she was staying with her family.

He was thirty-two, already famous as a writer and lecturer, and already under the spell of Livy's picture. He fell in love at once. She was twenty-two, still recovering from a long illness, and not ready to give her heart to any man, famous, amusing, and attentive as he might be. On New Year's Day Sam began the traditional round of social calls by calling first on Olivia. He stayed with her all day.

The more he knew of her the more devoted he became. She had been through a strange experience. After a hard fall ice skating at age sixteen she had been unable to get up. She was carried home to bed where she lay paralyzed for two years. Doctor after doctor was consulted. None could cure her or even explain her condition. Her parents very nearly gave up hope, but as a last resort they brought a faith healer to her bedside. After a short prayer, the healer miraculously lifted Livy to a sitting position and later moved her to a chair. Sensation slowly returned to her numb legs, and within a few days she began to walk again.

Already deeply religious, the experience had strengthened her faith. She thought every right-thinking person should believe in God. Sam Clemens didn't. And he was so unconventional no one, not even Sam himself, could predict what he might say. This could be disturbing.

And he had an unconventional appearance. His second-hand, travel-wrinkled clothes, his unruly hair, touched with gray, his lazy way of talking, combined with the strong smell of tobacco, did not exactly fill a maiden's dreams. Jervis Langdon, Olivia's father, liked Sam immediately, but Olivia confessed that she was at first more fascinated than charmed.

During the holidays Sam also called on Reverend Beecher, organizer of the *Quaker City* trip, and met members of his family, including Harriet Beecher Stowe, author of *Uncle Tom's Cabin*, the influential antislavery novel. The Beechers gave Sam some tips on dealing with publishers.

When Sam returned to Washington early in January, he found that a friend, acting without his knowledge, had committed him to give a lecture. "I hardly knew what I was going to talk about," he wrote his mother, "but it went off in splendid style." He talked, undoubtedly after much rehearsal, about the Holy Land excursion.

Soon after the talk he went to Hartford to meet his publisher. Although accustomed to authors of more polished manner and dress, Bliss soon saw that behind the tobacco smoke and the wrinkled clothes was a genius.

He gave Sam the choice of a ten-thousand-dollar flat payment for his manuscript or a 5 percent royalty on sales. Sam decided on royalties and later said it was the best business decision he ever made.

He went back to Washington and set to work. Friends, fooled by his languid pose, were always astounded at Mark Twain's capacity for work. He worked day in and day out, adding chapter after chapter until disturbing news from California stopped him short.

The editors of the *Alta* had decided to publish their collection of Sam's letters from the *Quaker City* voyage. Sam telegraphed a protest, but the reply was not satisfactory. The *Alta*, it seemed, had legal rights to the letters.

Sam sailed for California. To his delight, he received a hero's welcome everywhere. It began at the Isthmus of Panama where a delegation came to the dock to welcome him. On the other side, he boarded a ship commanded by his old friend Ned Wakeman. The two enjoyed a warm reunion.

In San Francisco, the editors of the *Alta*, admitting that they had already benefited greatly from Sam's letters, released the copyright to him. Sam, for his part, promised to give the paper full credit for financing the trip.

Then he went before a San Francisco audience.

"I lectured here on the trip the other night," he wrote Bliss. "Over sixteen hundred dollars gold in the house—every seat taken & paid for. . . ."

He stayed in California to finish the manuscript. Some letters had to be heavily revised, others even eliminated. When he finished late in June he followed his old lecture tour through California and Nevada. Again, he was warmly received by audiences everywhere. He came back to San Francisco for his final talk on July 2. Four days later he sailed for New York.

The trip took twenty-three days, and soon after he landed, he made his way to Hartford to deliver the manuscript to Bliss. It had sixty-two chapters and was called *The New Pilgrims' Progress*.

Bliss accepted the book eagerly, but his board of directors objected to the title which seemed to make fun of John Bunyan's famous seventeenth-century allegory, *The Pilgrim's Progress*. Did this mean the book was irreverent? And what about Mark Twain himself? Was he a Christian?

After Bliss threatened to resign, the board agreed to publish the book if the title were changed. Eventually, *The Innocents Abroad, or The New Pilgrims' Progress* won general approval.

While the book was being readied for publication, Sam got down to serious courtship. Ostensibly, he went to Elmira, New York, to visit Charley Langdon, but Sam really wanted to see Olivia again. Charley, who met him at the station, was dismayed to find Sam in a wrinkled and travel-stained suit.

Sam had packed a fresh outfit, however, and when he appeared before the family, he was properly groomed and dressed. He stayed a week. Susan Crane, Livy's older sister, saw at once that Sam was in love, but Charley had to be told, and it upset him. He worshipped Livy. No one was worthy of her.

Charley urged Sam to leave at once, but Sam found a way to delay his departure. It happened when a loose seat in the carriage taking him to the train station tipped and dumped him on the street. Sam feigned injury and stayed with the Langdons two more days.

All through the courtship, Sam's pen flowed. He barraged Livy with love notes and letters, often taking the role of a disappointed swain.

. . . For I do not regret that I have loved you, still love & shall always love you. I accept the situation, uncomplainingly, hard as it is. Of old I am acquainted with grief, disaster & disappointment & have borne these troubles as became a man. So, also, I shall bear this last & bitterest, even though it break my heart. . . . It is better to have loved & lost you than that my life should have remained forever the blank it was before. . . .

When Sam finally left Elmira he went to Cleveland, Ohio, to visit his former traveling companion Mary Fairbanks and then to St. Louis where he stayed with his family for several days. He wrote to Livy once, sometimes twice a day.

His next stop was Hartford where he stayed with Bliss and his family while correcting proof sheets for *Innocents*. It was a happy visit. Mrs. Bliss introduced him to her many friends and took him to church socials and other gatherings.

Hartford was a wealthy town, and Sam slyly named the recently completed Congregational church "The Church of the Holy Speculators." Sam soon made friends with its energetic pastor. The Reverend Joseph Hopkins Twichell's keen mind, quick wit, and sense of humor matched Sam's personality perfectly. Although he did not have Twichell's strong religious faith, Sam respected it. For his part, Twichell made no effort to change his new friend's philosophy.

Twichell introduced Sam to Harmony, his new wife, and the two of them encouraged Sam to marry and settle down. Sam confessed, according to Twichell, that he was "in love beyond all telling with the dearest and best girl in the world."

Meanwhile, the need for illustrations had delayed publication of the book, and Sam decided to lecture to raise some much-needed money.

He began a busy schedule in the fall of 1868 and continued

on the tour well into the following spring. His talk, called "The American Vandal Abroad," was well received, and each time he spoke, he earned at least one hundred dollars. He once more sent money regularly to his mother.

The tour added to Mark Twain's stature as a rustic philosopher and a humorist. One reporter called him a "lion" and "the coming man of the age."

Another reporter described Mark Twain as "a man of medium height, about five feet ten, sparsely built, with dark reddish-brown hair and mustache. His features are fair, his eyes keen and twinkling. He dresses in scrupulous evening attire. In lecturing he hangs about the desk, leaning on it or flirting around the corners of it, then marching and counter-marching in the rear of it. He seldom casts a glance at his manuscript." He spoke with a "long, monotonous drawl, with the fun invariably coming at the end of a sentence—after a pause."[2]

Sam's "manuscript" consisted of nothing more than crude drawings or symbols to guide his memory and prevent omissions. Because many of his lectures were in central New York State, he visited the Langdons often and he made progress. On November 26 and 27, 1868, he wrote Mrs. Fairbanks to announce that Livy had agreed to marry him, and that he was "so happy I am almost beside myself."

Next day to Twichell:

Sound the loud timbrel!—& let yourself out to your most prodigious capacity,—for I have fought the good fight & lo! I have won! Refused three times—warned to *quit* once—accepted at last!

Livy's parents, Jervis and Olivia Langdon, liked Sam but

withheld immediate approval of marriage. As Sam told his mother and Pamela,

> When I am permanently *settled*—& when I am a Christian—& when I have *demonstrated* that I have a good, steady, reliable character, her parents will withdraw their objections, & she may marry me. . . .

Olivia's father wrote some of Sam's friends for references. Meanwhile, Theodore Crane, married to Olivia's older sister, endorsed Sam enthusiastically, and after hearing from Sam's friends, her father withdrew all objections. The engagement was formally announced on February 4, 1869.

Some of the Langdons' conservative friends said Livy was unwise to marry anyone who had worked as a printer, a riverboat pilot, a miner, and a stage personality.

Sam was too happy to care what anyone said. He wrote his mother about Livy:

> She is only a little body, but she hasn't her peer in Christendom. I gave her only a plain gold engagement ring, when fashion imperatively demands a two-hundred dollar diamond one—& told her it was typical of her future lot—namely that she would have to flourish on substantials, rather than luxuries (But you see I know the girl—she don't care anything about luxuries . . . One seldom sees a diamond about her.) She spends no money but her usual year's allowance, & she spends nearly every cent of that on other people. She will be a good sensible little wife, without any airs about her.

13

CHAPTER

The Newlyweds

Habit is habit, and not to be flung out the window by any man,
but coaxed down-stairs a step at a time.

Although Sam had a Christian background, his philosophy did
not fit traditional Christian beliefs. Friends who respected him
and accepted him as a freethinker did not always respect or
accept what he thought. This was the case with Olivia and her
family. They adored Sam, but many of his ideas upset them.
Sam tried to adjust.

He went to church with the Langdons, bowed his head at
meals when her father said grace, and read passages of the Bible
aloud with Livy. He even tried to give up swearing, something
friends said he had learned to do extremely well.

He had no trouble adopting the Langdons' strong abolitionist tradition. Prior to the war, Livy's family had long been active
in the underground railway, providing a haven for escaped
slaves and helping them find their way into Canada. Even
though Sam's family had owned slaves, and even though he

104

served briefly in a Confederate militia, Sam had already made up his mind that slavery was one of man's worst evils.

Livy made fun of Sam's exuberance and impetuous nature. She began calling him "Youth," and urged him to be more deliberate in what he said and wrote. He tried. In fact, it may have been Livy who encouraged him to hold his letters for a few days before mailing them, particularly letters he had written in anger.

He obliged Livy in his wardrobe, giving up his untidy, wrinkled ensemble to become an immaculate dresser. As in his piloting days, he once again took pride in his appearance.

He also respected Livy's literary tastes and frequently deferred to her judgment. Today, some scholars argue that Livy's influence as chief critic and editor distorted Sam's work. But she was also his chief inspiration. Without her encouragement and guidance, he might not have written as much or as well.

During March 1869, after leaving the lecture circuit, Sam and Livy read the proofs for *The Innocents Abroad*. It was a great relief to be settled. He had "gone on the platform," as he called it, some fifty times in less than six months. Although he had earned about eight thousand dollars, he had traveled constantly and repeated the same talk over and over until he was sick of it. He said he would never go lecturing again.

He and Olivia made several changes that further delayed publication of *Innocents Abroad*. Finally, however, in July 1869, twenty thousand copies of the book were printed and offered at an average price of about $3.50 each. It was an immediate bestseller. Another press run had to be ordered at once, then another. After twelve months, sales passed sixty-nine thousand, and the pace continued at one thousand or more new orders each month. No travel book had ever been so successful.

Although the book poked fun at Old World pretensions and

traditions, it did so with such candor and good fun that few readers could take offense. Copies by the untold thousands sold in Europe, but these were all pirated editions. Sam received no royalties, but the praise from both sides of the Atlantic was glowing. William Dean Howells, one of America's most respected novelists and editors, lauded Mark Twain in the pages of the *Atlantic Monthly.*

All this might have given Sam further literary ambitions, but he did not see a future in authorship. He thought of himself simply as a newspaper man who had been lucky enough to write a popular book. In fact, he wanted to get back to the newspaper business by buying a paper. During his lecture tour, he came close to acquiring an interest in the *Cleveland Herald,* but it was too far from Elmira. Then he learned he could buy one-third interest in the *Buffalo Express.* That was closer, but the price was twenty-five thousand dollars. He was ready to go lecturing again to raise the money, but then Livy's father offered to cover most of the purchase with a loan. Sam went to work on the *Express* on August 14, 1869.

In his introductory editorial Sam declared:

I only wish to assure parties having a friendly interest in the prosperity of the journal, that I am not going to hurt the paper deliberately and intentionally at any time. I am not going to introduce any startling reforms, nor in any way attempt to make trouble. . . . I shall not make use of slang or vulgarity upon any occasion or under any circumstances, and shall never use profanity except in discussing house-rent and taxes. Indeed, upon a second thought, I will not even use it then, for it is unchristian, inelegant, and degrading: though—to speak truly I do not see how house-rent and taxes are going to be discussed worth a cent without it. I shall not often meddle with politics, because we have a political editor who is already excellent, and only needs to serve a term in the penitentiary to be perfect. I shall not write any poetry unless I conceive a spite against the subscribers. . . .[1]

He had acquired two partners, Colonel George F. Selkirk, the business manager, and Josephus N. Larned, political editor. Both believed Mark Twain's reputation would bring in more subscribers. Certainly, whatever he wrote would make the paper more entertaining. Sam's early contributions, however, were mostly light and brief.

He and Livy wanted to marry in December, but he had to have more cash first and he asked James Redpath, head of the Boston Lyceum Bureau, the best agency of the day, to book lectures in and around New England. He opened in Boston on November 10, and used Redpath's Boston office as his headquarters during the next several weeks.

During this period he met William Dean Howells, then assistant editor of the *Atlantic Monthly*. Unlike Sam, William Dean Howells was shy and retiring. Son of an Ohio printer, Howells had become a successful novelist after serving briefly in Venice, Italy, as American consul. Unlike the slow-talking Sam, Howells could be mistaken for a New Englander. But Sam respected Howells's experience and ability and the two became lifelong friends. Sam benefited greatly from Howells's literary judgment, guidance, and encouragement.

Meanwhile, to Sam's surprise, Redpath had booked lectures well into January. This forced the delay of the wedding until February 2, 1870. Actually, the delay gave Sam time to search for a boardinghouse in Buffalo where he and Livy could begin their married life.

He thought that a friend had found a place for them when

William Dean Howells

he appeared at the Langdons' late in January. Livy and her generous parents, however, had prepared a surprise. The Langdons had bought and furnished a house for the newlyweds on Delaware Avenue, one of Buffalo's finest residential streets. It was even staffed with servants.

The evening wedding took place in the Langdons' Elmira home with the Reverends Joseph Twichell and Thomas K. Beecher, half brother of Henry Ward Beecher, officiating before some one hundred guests. Sam's sister, Pamela Moffett, now a widow, and her daughter, Annie, now a grown woman, had come from St. Louis. Mary Fairbanks had come from Cleveland.

Dancing followed a wedding supper, but the affair was quiet and sedate. The following afternoon, the Langdons put the newlyweds on the train for Buffalo. When a friend met them at the station with a sleigh, Sam, still unsuspecting, thought they would go to the boardinghouse. Instead, they turned onto Delaware Avenue and stopped before a new, brightly lit house. The house, one of the finest on the street, was occupied, full of people, in fact.

Even when they entered the house, Sam remained confused until Livy explained. For one of the few times in his life, he stood speechless. After Livy handed him the deed to the house, Sam still could not find his voice. The housewarming party was well under way before he regained his composure and began to express his gratitude.

It was a promising beginning for a marriage. He and Livy settled into their new home with high spirits. At work, he filled the office with good cheer. Larned, who shared the same work-table with him, recalled that Sam seemed to enjoy every moment. He frequently laughed out loud as he worked, and he worked long and hard, sometimes arriving at eight A.M. and staying until ten o'clock at night.

He was generally liked, seemed unconscious of his fame, and put everyone at ease. Usually he took off his tie before he sat down to work. Sometimes he even kicked off his shoes.

He focused on humorous pieces at first, but soon began writing more serious articles. When Larned was absent, he wrote editorials, often with apology. One of his first began, "I do not know much about politics and am not sitting up nights to learn. . . ."

He was quick to defend the oppressed and disadvantaged and attack those who used them. Sincere and zealous, he championed liberty and justice without trying to be funny or entertaining.

News of Anson Burlingame's death in Russia on February 23, 1870, prompted a heartfelt tribute from Sam who praised the diplomat's long service to the public and his personal friendship and influence.

Sam also wrote articles for a New York magazine, which gave him an annual retainer of two thousand dollars. In one of these Sam questioned the Christian charity of a minister who complained that working-class families in the pews of fashionable churches drove away families of the better class. Later, after another class-conscious minister refused to give the burial service for a famous actor, Sam wrote a stout defense of the acting profession and attacked the prejudice against it.

In yet another article, Sam raged at the cruel treatment of the Chinese in San Francisco. Later he wrote a series of letters purporting to be from a Chinese immigrant who was beaten, attacked by dogs, jailed, and convicted without fair trial soon after his arrival in the "promised land."

Livy ran a Christian household. When Joe Goodman came from Nevada to visit the newlyweds, he was shocked by Sam's apparent piety. Mornings began with prayers and Bible reading. Grace was said before every meal. This was not the Sam Clemens that Goodman remembered.

As the months passed, Sam gradually gave up the pretense of the rituals and became more confident in speaking his mind on religious matters. For her part, Livy grew more tolerant and sympathetic to some of Sam's unorthodox opinions.

They went to few parties and entertained rarely. When a new couple moved into the house across the street, Sam and

A miniature watercolor on cardboard of Olivia, made in 1864, was still in Sam's possession at the time of his death.

Livy were slow to make the welcoming visit expected in those days. It was not until Sam saw smoke coming from an upstairs window of the newcomers' house, that he crossed the street.

"My name is Clemens," he reportedly said. "We ought to have called on you before, and I beg your pardon for intruding now in this informal way, but your house is on fire."[2]

Sam and Livy might have become more social if illness had not unsettled their lives. In June 1870 Jervis Langdon became so sick that the newlyweds had to rush to Elmira to help care for him. Nursing continued around the clock. Sam took the midnight-to-four A.M. shifts and sat with his father-in-law again for an hour or two during the day. The weeks passed slowly until Jervis Langdon died on August 6, 1870. He left his family physically and emotionally exhausted.

Livy, pregnant by now, was visited by an old friend after she and Sam returned to Buffalo. Emma Nye had hardly settled into the house on Delaware Avenue, however, when she fell ill with typhoid fever. Despite constant attention from Sam and Livy, Miss Nye died on September 29. Livy, now ill herself, gave premature birth to a son on November 7. It was hardly a joyful occasion. Little Langdon Clemens seemed to be in jeopardy from the start, and Livy herself was seriously ill. Both mother and baby, however, gradually gained strength. Life slowly returned to normal.

Through all these troubles, Bliss had been urging Sam to write another book. *The Innocents Abroad* continued to break sales records, and Bliss wanted to introduce another book while public interest in Mark Twain was still high.

For a time, Sam worked on a yarn that treated Noah's voyage on the ark as a travel cruise with a full complement of biblical characters. But the work went slowly, and Bliss wanted a new manuscript within the year. How about Sam's western adventures?

Sam liked the idea, and the regular royalty checks from *Innocents* had convinced him that he might have a future in authorship after all. Also, Sam's association with the *Express* had not boosted its circulation as much as expected, and he realized he had lost his enthusiasm for the paper. Before 1870 drew to a close, he and Livy talked of selling his interest in the paper, selling their home, and moving to Hartford.

They liked Hartford for several reasons. For one thing, Orion and Mollie now lived there. Through Sam's influence, Orion had gone to work editing a literary paper that Bliss had recently begun publishing. Sam also liked the idea of having the Congregational minister Joseph Twichell and his wife Harmony and other friends as neighbors. Furthermore, Hartford offered the intellectual stimulation Sam needed.

Sam had written Orion asking for help in remembering the stage trip and their adventures in Nevada. Orion, as might be imagined, set to work assiduously. Sam meanwhile was distracted by a recently discovered diamond mine in South Africa. He made arrangements with a newspaper friend who would go to South Africa, investigate, and take notes. Then he and the friend would collaborate on a book about the mine.

Soon after, the friend returned with volumes of notes; however, he died of cancer and Sam had to give up the project.

In April 1871 Sam sold his interest in the *Express* for fifteen thousand dollars. This was ten thousand dollars less than he had paid, but he was willing to accept the loss in order to get away from Buffalo.

He immediately took Livy and the baby to Elmira to stay with Theodore and Susan Crane, Livy's sister, at their hilltop retreat called Quarry Farm. Thus began a series of happy and productive summers.

14

Home and Abroad

Adam and Eve had every advantage, but the principal one is that they escaped teething.

An abandoned limestone quarry gave the farm its name, and the hilltop location gave it relief from summer heat as well as a panoramic view of Elmira and the Chemung River.

Sam and Livy had planned a brief stay, but a few days in the relaxed atmosphere and the Cranes' love and hospitality changed their minds. It was a grand summer. Both Livy and little Langdon gained strength. And Sam, enjoying boundless energy and enthusiasm, had some of the most productive days of his life.

For a time he thought of giving up the western book, but when Joe Goodman arrived from Nevada and praised what Sam had written so far, he went to work with zeal. Goodman agreed to extend his visit. He helped Sam recall the Nevada experiences, and he read the new manuscript pages at the end of every day. He said Sam had never done better work.

With his old friend's encouragement, Sam added thirty to

sixty-five manuscript pages each day. It is astounding that he had energy left over for other projects. When a magazine offered him six thousand dollars for twelve articles on any subject, he accepted and filled the assignment before summer's end. He also contributed sketches for Bliss's Hartford paper and somehow found time to take brief trips to Hartford and New York.

On top of all this, Sam recorded his first invention, a self tightening vest strap which was clever but not profitable.

Meanwhile, he gave in to Redpath's insistence and agreed to join the winter lecture circuit. He requested, however, that Redpath not book him in churches because audiences seemed afraid to laugh there. Sam prepared three new lectures, one based on his western book, another on various characters he had known, and the third a tribute to Artemus Ward who had died in 1867.

From Quarry Farm, Sam took Livy and the baby to Hartford and got them settled in a rented house before he left for Boston. Sam lectured only because he needed money, first to repay the balance on the loan from the Langdon family after the sale of the *Buffalo Express,* and then to build a house. Sam and Livy had decided by now to spend the rest of their days in Hartford.

Mark Twain opened in Bethlehem, Pennsylvania, on October 16, 1871. Another lecture and another town followed, and another, and another. It seemed endless. Fortunately, many of his bookings were close to home, making frequent visits to Hartford possible.

He soon dropped the talk about various characters he had known and spoke either about Ward or his western adventures. He used his characteristic opening. Instead of having the usual introduction by a member of the local lecture committee, Sam introduced himself. He came on pretending to be a local committeeman and delighted his audiences when he abruptly changed roles and became Mark Twain.

He still managed, through his informal style and long, thoughtful pauses, to mesmerize his audiences. After one lecture, a man complained that Sam had not talked for even ten minutes and could hardly be convinced otherwise even though his watch showed that more than an hour had passed.

Other speakers on Redpath's circuit that season included Henry Ward Beecher, editor Horace Greeley, and humorists Josh Billings and Petroleum V. Nasby. Whenever any of them were in Boston, they stayed at Young's Hotel. There, Sam could put his feet up, puff on his pipe, and enjoy the company of his fellow speakers. He sometimes saw his old friend from California, Bret Harte, who had won fame with such stories as "The Outcasts of Poker Flat" and "The Luck of Roaring Camp." Harte had come to Boston to work with William Dean Howells on the *Atlantic Monthly*.

Before February 1872 drew to a close, Sam, with his final lecture behind him, settled down to enjoy the comfort of his home and the affection of his family and friends. The western book, now called *Roughing It,* went on sale soon after.

It combined passages of fine description with outrageous fun, humor, and exaggeration, giving a valuable record of Sam's personal experiences during a unique period in our history. Although he sometimes strayed from the facts, his story stuck close to the spirit of the time and the region.

Roughing It enjoyed critical acclaim and brisk sales, but it did not match the success of *Innocents Abroad.* One hundred thousand copies of that book sold in three years. It took ten years to sell that many copies of *Roughing It.*

Sam took one thousand dollars out of his initial royalties

and sent it to Orion for providing his remembrances for the book. Orion needed the money. His employment with Bliss had been brief, and he and Mollie were now back in Keokuk.

Sam and Livy's second child, Olivia Susan Clemens, to be known as Susy, was born on March 19, 1872. She was a healthy baby, but little Langdon remained tragically weak. He died on June 2, age eighteen months, probably of diphtheria. Sam blamed himself for Langdon's death.

He had taken the child for a carriage ride one cold morning, and failed to notice when the boy's blanket slipped off him. The brief exposure, he felt, had started the fatal illness, and Sam could not forgive himself.

After this, Sam and Livy felt they needed a change of scene, so instead of going to Quarry Farm, that summer they took Susan to Saybrook on the Connecticut coast. While there, Sam invented a scrapbook with pregummed pages. To glue something into the book, it was only necessary to moisten the gum. No messy paste pot was needed.

Dan Slote, his old *Quaker City* cabin mate, took the idea and produced the popular Mark Twain scrapbook. It was Sam's only successful invention. Unfortunately, Sam would later accuse Slote of keeping more than his share of profits. Their friendship ended, but sales of the scrapbook continued well into the twentieth century.

During the same summer, Sam's interest in protecting his literary rights prompted a trip to England. He and Bliss had gone to the unusual trouble of getting an English copyright for *Roughing It*. This led to legitimate publication by a London firm and prevented pirate editions. Now Sam thought he might benefit by doing the same thing with *Innocents Abroad* and his anthology of short stories. He also thought the trip might give him enough material for another travel book.

With Livy and five-month-old Susy safely back at Hartford, Sam sailed alone for England on August 21, 1872. He was somewhat puzzled at first by the reserve of the English people. On the train from Liverpool to London, he spotted a fellow passenger reading *Roughing It* without the faintest hint of a smile.

Sam soon learned, however, that such reserve was part of the English charm, and his long love affair with England began. And the English people, once they discovered him, became fascinated with Mark Twain.

Sam happened to arrive at the office of his British publishers in time to join an editorial luncheon. While Sam talked, the editors listened. They listened while lunch was served. They listened as they ate, and long after the plates were cleared, they sat listening. Teatime came and went, but no one left the room. Night was falling when the "luncheon" meeting finally adjourned.

Sam's reputation spread through London like a windblown fire. He soon found himself at parties where statesmen, politicians, artists, authors, actors, and members of the English aristocracy all wanted to meet him and hear him talk. Hostesses vied to put Mark Twain on their guest lists. He spent most weekends at someone's country home. When he was not out, people called on him at his hotel.

He was expected to speak at banquets and never disappointed anyone. Loud applause greeted him as soon as he stood. He discovered that the English loved to be teased. Once when chided for carrying a cheap, cotton umbrella, he said it was the only model he could find that an Englishman would not steal. This response was repeated the next day all over London.

The English reception was warmer and more enthusiastic than any he had received at home, and indeed, the English appreciated Mark Twain's literary genius when most American readers still regarded him as one of several western humorists. Sam established several lifelong friendships during his visit.

"I came here to take notes for a book," he wrote his mother, "but I haven't done much but attend dinners and make speeches. I have had a jolly good time, and I do hate to go away from these English folks; they make a stranger feel entirely at home, and they laugh so easily that it is a comfort to make after-dinner speeches here. I have made hundreds of friends. . . ."

He put aside, for the moment, his idea for a travel book on England. He respected the people too much to poke fun at and ridicule them. He sailed for home on November 12, 1872, knowing he would return.

Although Sam gave a few talks for charity, he turned down Redpath's pleas to go on the lecture circuit that winter. He wanted to enjoy his family and his new Hartford friends. Meanwhile, his success in England had increased his stature at home. He spoke to members of New York's Lotos Club and accepted their invitation to join.

With Livy and Susy in good health, the Clemenses entered Hartford's busy social life. Their own house soon became a popular gathering place where neighbors could arrive unannounced. Sam encouraged the informality. Some friends came in without even knocking.

Novelist Charles Dudley Warner and his wife became good friends, and over dinner one February evening in 1873, Warner and Sam criticized the novels their wives were reading. Livy and Susan Warner challenged the men to write something better, and they promptly accepted the challenge.

Sam had never collaborated and never written pure fiction before, but in a flood of enthusiasm, he dashed off eleven chapters of a story with a central character modeled after James Lampton, his mother's cousin, whose unfailing optimism and unending get-rich schemes had become a family joke. Lampton lived on hope and talked with such conviction that his listeners often forgot that the man himself had never succeeded at anything.

Sam's plot turned on the elusive promise of the Tennessee land. Warner added twelve chapters before turning the story back to Sam. This continued until April. Three months of work had produced a book that they called *The Gilded Age.* It had many faults, but Colonel Eschol Sellers, the fabulous central character, caught Sam's fancy and would inspire further stories. Furthermore, the book gave him training in modeling fictional characters on real people and plots on real experiences. He would repeat this practice again and again with stunning success.

Sam and Livy, meanwhile, purchased a building lot on Hartford's Farmington Avenue and began planning their home. It would be a large house with a peaceful view of a willow-shaded stream that flowed across the bottom of the property.

In May, with the site cleared, and the plans in a builder's hands, Sam took his family to England. Clara Spaulding, one of Livy's closest friends, sailed with them to help her care for Susy who was barely a year old. Sam had hoped to write, but social engagements kept him far too busy.

They rented a suite in the Langham Hotel where lords and ladies and London's leading literary figures lined up to call on them. The poet Robert Browning and Lewis Carroll, author of *Alice in Wonderland,* were among those who enjoyed Mark Twain's wit and Livy's friendly spirit.

The Clemenses were treated like royalty, but the pace was exhausting. Late in July they went to Edinburgh, Scotland, to give Livy some much-needed rest. Insisting that she have a medical examination, Sam found Dr. John Brown, who turned out to be the author of the popular "Rab and His Friends," an enchanting dog story. Dr. Brown not only put Livy on the road to rest and recovery, but also became the family's enthusiastic guide, Sam's literary companion, and a longtime friend and correspondent.

Livy loved Scotland, in spite of the inevitable round of teas and dinners. They all left with regret, and even after two weeks in Ireland and another two weeks in Paris, Edinburgh remained Livy's favorite city. She was now ready for home, but Sam had promised to give six London lectures.

The talks, which opened on the night of October 13, 1873, in the city's largest auditorium, were a huge success. A packed audience heard about "Our Fellow Savages of the Sandwich Islands" and laughed louder and clapped longer than any audience Sam had entertained.

Moved by the enthusiastic response, Sam agreed to return to London for several more lectures as soon as he could settle his family safely at home.

They landed in New York on November 2. Orion, now a proofreader for a New York publisher, met them and described a flying machine he had recently invented and a novel he was currently writing. He wanted Sam to give him some tips on lecturing. Sam, however, was too anxious to get to Hartford to give Orion and his fantasies much attention.

Indeed, Sam did have a tight schedule. He was soon back in London, speaking again before large crowds, but this time his subject was the American West. He hoped that his talks might promote sales of *Roughing It.*

His London friends kept him busy with many engagements. He was always a willing after-dinner speaker, and before he left, he was invited to join the prestigious Athenaeum Club, an honor just short of knighthood.

Sam returned to Hartford on January 13, 1874, and faced a troubling problem. In *The Gilded Age,* he and Warner had given their lead character the unusual name of Colonel Eschol Sellers, never dreaming that there was a real person with a similar name. And now George Eschol Sellers in the flesh threatened to sue for ten thousand dollars. Only after Bliss withdrew all outstanding copies of the book and changed the character's name to Beriah Sellers in subsequent editions, did the real Sellers drop his demands.

Meanwhile, *The Gilded Age* had become a financial if not a critical success. It had been issued in December and was already in its third edition. Sam decided to try more fiction, this time without a collaborator.

15

Tom Sawyer

"Classic." A book which people praise and don't read.

Mark Twain was already famous by the time he started writing *The Adventures of Tom Sawyer,* famous and fast becoming wealthy. His books were successful by every measure; whenever he lectured he drew standing-room audiences; and he had even made modest showing as an inventor.

Now he wanted to enjoy his success and his wealth. The new home would be one of the largest in Hartford. It was taking longer to build than expected, but it would be a showplace. He bought a chicken farm for Orion in Keokuk, and later, when that venture failed, Sam set up a pension fund for his brother. Although glad to be able to help, Sam sometimes lost patience.

To his mother he wrote, "I *can't* encourage Orion. Nobody can do that conscientiously, for the reason that before one's letter has time to reach him he is off on some new wild-goose chase. . . ."

At Quarry Farm the Cranes had built an author's retreat for

their now-famous brother-in-law, and they encouraged him to start using it in April. The little building, standing on the point of a hill, was comfortably furnished. It even had a small stove. Sam told Twichell:

> It is the loveliest study you ever saw. It is octagonal, with a peaked roof, each face lined with a spacious window, and it sits perched in complete isolation on the top of an elevation that commands leagues of valley and city and retreating ranges of distant blue hills. It is a cozy nest and just room in it for a sofa, table, and three or four chairs, and when the storms sweep down the remote valley and the lightning flashes behind the hills beyond, and the rain beats upon the roof over my head, imagine the luxury of it.

Sam was eager to begin work. For some time he had been planning a story based on his childhood in Hannibal. He still recalled his experiences and his friends of those days with pleasure. He would use his old friends and members of his family as models for the book. Of course, he made changes. Henry Clemens, for instance, had to be stripped of all his lovable qualities to become the goody-goody, despicable Sid.

Although he adjusted his characters to fit his story, the setting with the river and its islands, the cave, and the town of Hannibal went into the book with just one major change. Instead of Hannibal, Sam named it St. Petersburg.

Always most productive in the summer months, Sam went to his new study every morning soon after breakfast and stayed there all day. He rarely stopped for lunch and usually did not return to the house until about five in the evening. Livy and the Cranes could call him with a horn if they needed him during the day, but the horn rarely blew. Livy did not want him to work on Sundays, but he sometimes stole into his study for a few hours just the same.

This working routine was interrupted on June 8, 1874, by the arrival of Clara Langdon Clemens. Both mother and baby, however, came through the ordeal in good health, and the father soon returned to his book.

His output was prodigious. He wrote Dr. Brown in Scotland:

> I have been writing fifty pages of manuscript a day, on an average, for some time now, on a book (a story), and consequently have been so wrapped up in it, and dead to everything else, that I have fallen mighty short in letter writing. . . .
>
> On hot days I spread the study wide open, anchor my papers down with brickbats, and write in the midst of the hurricane, clothed in the same thin linen we make shirts of.

Actually, Sam continued to be a conscientious correspondent, but he could no longer answer much of his fan mail. Letters from hopeful authors asking his advice or his opinion on manuscripts were usually ignored. He made an exception when Orion began writing a book and sending installments. Sam sent back suggestions regularly until Orion switched to a different project.

Sam and his brother-in-law Theodore Crane enjoyed a common interest in travel and science books, histories, and literature. On Sunday afternoons, they often stretched out side by side on portable hammocks and read to each other from favorite books, including *The Diary of Samuel Pepys* and Richard Henry Dana, Jr.'s *Two Years Before the Mast*. Although fiction was not preferred during the day, they liked to read the novels of William Dean Howells aloud to the whole family after dinner.

Howells, by now a close friend, had been urging Sam to write for the *Atlantic Monthly.* Sam could not think of anything to do for the influential magazine until he found inspiration in the Quarry Farm household. That summer it included two nursemaids, two housemaids, a coachman, and a cook. The latter, Auntie Cord, sixty-eight years old, had lived her first forty years in slavery. She had once been sold for one thousand dollars, and she still boasted about it. Her children had all been sold from her, and she could not remember much about them.

Sam, with an acute ear for dialogue, simply interviewed Auntie Cord and wrote down what she said. He submitted "A True Story, Repeated Word for Word as I Heard It" without much hope. Auntie Cord's vocabulary and her way of speaking, after all, were not what readers of the *Atlantic* had grown to expect. Howells, however, bought the story immediately for sixty dollars and urged Sam to write more.

The Tom Sawyer story, however, had most of his attention, and when he finally interrupted that work, it was to take care of upsetting business. *The Gilded Age,* without authorization from Sam or Warner, had been adopted for the stage by Gilbert S. Dunsmore and was being readied for production in San Francisco with the popular John T. Raymond in the lead role.

Sam demanded by wire that production be stopped. A brisk exchange of letters followed. Dunsmore agreed to let Sam and Warner participate in the proceeds and even change the script if they wished.

Sam began writing his own stage version of the story without even waiting to see Dunsmore's script. Eventually, Dunsmore sold his interest to Sam and Warner. Raymond stayed with the project and played a delightful Colonel Sellers when the play opened that fall in New York. The production won critical raves, enjoyed a long run, and eventually earned some one hundred thousand dollars in royalties for the authors.

Late in the fall when the Clemenses moved into the new house at Hartford, workmen still had not completed some final touches. Sam and Livy, with many rooms to fill, spent several days buying furniture. The house was a curiosity. Unlike other Hartford homes, the kitchen faced the street. The front door was at one side of the house. There was a bedroom on the ground floor and a fireplace under a window. The Clemenses had a billiard room where the attic should be.

Billiards had become one of Sam's favorite pastimes. But he also enjoyed long walks with Joe Twichell. Talking constantly, the two friends could go miles from home without realizing it. Ten miles in one afternoon was not unusual.

Sometimes they hopped on the train to get home, or they might begin by train and then get off to walk home. On November 12, 1874, after much planning, they began a walk from Hartford to Boston. They managed twenty-eight miles that day, but Sam was too sore in the morning for much more. After hobbling along for six miles, he and Twichell went the rest of the way by train.

During one walk, after hearing about Sam's life as a river pilot, Twichell encouraged him to write it all down and submit the story to the *Atlantic*. Sam liked the suggestion enough to put the Tom Sawyer story aside once again. The Mississippi recollections, it soon became clear, could only be told with a series of articles. Howells accepted the first at once and asked for another each month for as long as Sam could keep writing them.

He turned out three in ten days, but to refresh his memory, he decided he and Howells must take a trip on the river. Years would pass, however, before he could make it. Meanwhile, the first installment of "Old Times on the Mississippi" appeared in the January 1875 issue. Six more followed. Their authenticity, freshness, and humor delighted readers, and they gave an accurate history of one era of American culture and commerce that might otherwise have become hopelessly shrouded in romantic haze.

Once again, Sam was victimized by pirates. There were countless unauthorized reprints of the articles. One Canadian publisher collected them for a popular book. Sam grew more impatient than ever for international laws that would protect authors.

About this time, the first typewriters appeared. Always interested in inventions, Sam enthusiastically acquired a model, telling his friends that it would revolutionize writing. He practiced faithfully and even typed some letters, but he could not adjust to the keyboard. "Blame my cats," he wrote Howells, "but this thing requires genius to work it just right." He soon returned to the pen, but he continued even here to experiment, trying many different fountain pens and pencils.

Sam still enjoyed a good prank. Once, author and editor Thomas Bailey Aldrich, another member of the New England literary set, made the mistake of asking for Sam's photograph. Sam began sending Aldrich one every day. Not content with this joke, Sam increased the shipment, eventually stuffing seventy in one envelope. After Aldrich laughingly threatened to have Sam arrested, the flood of photos trickled to a stop.

Although the Sellers play continued a long run, even coming to Hartford for two performances in January 1875, Sam himself, except for a few charity appearances, refused to return to the lecture stage.

He did speak in favor of voting rights for women to fellow members of Hartford's Monday Evening Club. He also spoke as honored guest at a spelling bee.

"I don't see any use in spelling a word right—and never did," he told the audience. "I mean I don't see any use in having a uniform and arbitrary way of spelling words. We might as well make all clothes alike and cook all dishes alike. Sameness is tiresome; variety is pleasing." He went on to describe a friend who had a refreshing way of spelling. "He always spells 'kow' with a capital 'K.' Now that is just as good as to spell it with a small one. . . ."

One morning in March 1875 Sam wrote his old friend William Wright, otherwise known as Dan De Quille, suggesting he write a history of the Nevada silver mines. The idea seemed inspired, but instead of mailing his letter, Sam put it aside in order to find out if Bliss would publish the history. While Sam's letter lay on his desk, a letter from Wright in far-off Nevada arrived. It outlined his plans for a history of the mines exactly as Sam had conceived it. Amazed at the coincidence, Sam urged Wright to come to Hartford at once and discuss the project with Bliss. *The Big Bonanza* was published a year later, receiving good reviews and paying handsome royalties to Wright.

In an article describing this experience, Sam coined the phrase "mental telegraphy," a phenomenon he believed in until the end of his days.

Bliss, meanwhile, had been pressing Sam for a new book, and the two agreed to put together a collection of articles, including his recent Auntie Cord story along with such old-timers as the jumping frog tale. The collection also included an open letter to Congress on copyright laws, perhaps the most serious piece, and a "translation" based on a French translation of the frog story, the funniest piece. Sam had turned the French version back into such awkward English that readers were left gasping with laughter after every sentence.

The collection itself, however, did not enjoy the sales that

Bliss and Sam anticipated. Meanwhile, he returned to *Tom Sawyer* and on July 5 wrote Howells:

> I have finished the story and didn't take the chap beyond boyhood. . . . If I went on now, and took him into manhood, he would just lie, like all the one-horse men of literature, and the reader would conceive a hearty contempt for him. It is not a boys' book at all. It will only be read by adults. It is only written for adults.

After reading the manuscript, however, Howells disagreed. "It is altogether the best story I ever read. It will be an immense success, but I think you ought to treat it explicitly *as* a boy's story. . . ."[1]

Sam took the advice, and before sending the manuscript to Bliss, revised it for younger readers.

16

The Author's Life

There are several good protections against temptations,
but the surest is cowardice.

Although he could not answer all his letters, the mail delighted him. Schoolchildren asked him for help with their compositions. Lovers even asked him for lyrics they could use in their wooing.

Some fans wrote to "Mark Twain, The United States" or "Mark Twain, The World." He received one letter addressed to "Mark Twain, God Knows Where?"

Some people wanted to make money on his name. He refused to let P. T. Barnum call his show "The Mark Twain Circus" and would not allow another to put his name on a collection of five thousand puns.

Perhaps the strangest request came from an English birdwatcher who wanted Sam to shoot, stuff, and ship 205 different species of American birds to England. Another Englishman started a Mark Twain club and regularly sent Sam minutes from club meetings and copies of speeches made by various members. Several years passed before Sam discovered that the club had no members, only the devoted fan who had started it.

Although avid readers knew that Mark Twain could be serious as well as funny, he was still generally classed as a humorist. For this reason, Sam left many articles unsigned. When he wrote in favor of voting rights for women, for instance, he knew that his article would not be taken seriously if it had Mark Twain's name on it.

Although his style seems effortless, in reality Sam wrote with difficulty. Many articles and stories, begun with enthusiasm, were never finished. Some beginnings were put aside for months and even years before he looked at them again. It was rare for him to carry an idea through from beginning to end at one time.

After working alone in his retreat at Quarry Farm all day, Sam returned to the house eager for company. Dinners gave him a chance to perform before an audience he loved. To the delight of his family and any guests who might be present, Sam talked and talked. Sometimes he got up between courses to walk and gesture broadly as he expressed himself.

After dinner, he usually read aloud what he had written during the day. He wanted suggestions, but was particularly sensitive to Livy's responses. Sometimes a lack of enthusiasm from her was enough to kill Sam's interest in a project.

"The Autobiography of a Damn Fool," based on Orion Clemens's life, was one of these. "Livy wouldn't have it so I gave up," Sam explained. In addition to her religious bias, Livy objected to profanity and any mention of sex or other biological functions.

At Hartford, Sam spoke at the Monday Evening Club and acted in the town's amateur theater productions. His fellow actors found Sam unreliable. As often as not, he would wander from the script, causing confusion on the stage and laughter in the audience.

When in Boston, Sam stayed with the Howellses, filling their home with tobacco smoke and disrupting their schedule. He usually stayed up late, talking or reading. The Howellses stayed up to listen, but they were also reluctant to retire ahead of their guest for fear that he might fall asleep with a lighted cigar or pipe.

The Adventures of Tom Sawyer was to come out early in 1876, but Sam delayed publication with the hope of blocking the Canadian book pirates. He had thwarted the British pirates by selling rights to a legitimate London printing house. He tried but failed to make a similar arrangement in Canada. The book finally came out in December 1876, and pirate editions went on sale in Canada soon after.

Meanwhile, Sam started a sequel to *Tom Sawyer*. It moved slowly.

"I like it tolerably well, as far as I have gone," he wrote a friend, "and may possibly pigeonhole or burn the manuscript when I am done." The story did languish for several years.

It was the story based on Bence Blankenship's attempt to shelter a runaway slave. Although the Civil War was over, slavery and racial issues were still volatile. Sam wanted to waken the American conscience to these issues without reviving old angers. He did not want to be rushed.

He turned to lighter things, including a brief farce set in Queen Elizabeth's court that begins when an unknown courtier breaks wind with such thunder that it cannot be ignored. The queen interrogates Shakespeare, Ben Jonson, Francis Bacon, Walter Raleigh, and others, not to chastise, but to honor the flatulent genius.

Sam called it *1601* and showed it to several male friends, including author and statesman John Hay who was probably the first to have it privately printed. It was reprinted again and again and eventually gained wide, underground circulation. Livy, of course, knew nothing of the work.

His working routine was often interrupted. Sam spoke at a Hartford rally for Rutherford B. Hayes, the Republican candidate for president. The artist Frank Millet came to Hartford to paint Sam's portrait. Bret Harte came to collaborate on a play with Sam. Although they finished it, the play was not a success, and the collaboration strained their friendship beyond repair.

This was one of the few friendships Sam could not maintain. Perhaps it was inevitable. Both men had made their marks in the West before joining the eastern literary establishment. Harte, whose stories usually had happy or surprise endings, fit more readily into literary traditions. He was easily accepted. Mark Twain, however, with his unorthodox beliefs, wide-ranging talent, and bold nature, was unpredictable. Although generally liked, he was not entirely trusted, particularly by conservative authors and critics.

The Adventures of Tom Sawyer, when it finally appeared, broke down much of the reserve. Critics and readers agreed that it appealed to everyone, not just to boys. It captured the free spirit of youth, the thirst for adventure, and the lust for rebellion that is part of everyone's childhood. And by unwinding his tale in a drowsy river town, Sam had written a uniquely American story.

At Quarry Farm, in the summer of 1877, Sam started *Simon Wheeler, the Amateur Detective,* a play. It had many funny lines and a clever plot, but Sam could find no one to produce it and put it aside to work on more stories and articles.

At this time Sam read Charlotte Yonge's *The Little Duke*

about Richard, Duke of Normandy, in tenth-century France. The book sent Sam's imagination soaring. Why not have a young prince and a look-alike beggar change roles?

That summer at Quarry Farm, working with a map of London close at hand, Sam wrote about four hundred manuscript pages of *The Prince and the Pauper*. His prince would be the son of Henry VIII who actually ruled under regents as Edward VI in the sixteenth century. When Sam returned to Hartford that fall, he put the book aside to work on other projects.

Sam had been asked to speak at a dinner honoring John Greenleaf Whittier on his seventieth birthday. It seemed the perfect occasion to poke fun at some of the leading contemporaries of American literature who would attend the banquet. For his speech, Sam chose a rustic western saloon as his scene and populated it with such "tramps" as Henry Wadsworth Longfellow, Ralph Waldo Emerson, and Oliver Wendell Holmes. Sam thought it hilarious, but if he had shown it to Livy, she might have warned him that the Bostonians would not appreciate his rollicking farce.

The speech was a disaster. Long before the talk ended, Howells recalled "there fell a silence weighing many tons to the square inch, which deepened from moment to moment, and was broken only by the hysterical and blood-curdling laughter of one guest whose name shall not be handed down to infamy."[1]

At first puzzled and then devastated, Sam returned to Hartford humiliated. His anguish kept him awake at nights. Livy did not help. When she heard about his speech, she simply agreed that he had made a serious mistake. He wrote Howells saying that he no longer expected his work to appear in the *Atlantic* because his name would hurt the magazine's reputation.

Although Howells agreed that the speech had been unfortunate, he said friends would forgive him and Mark Twain would always be welcome in the *Atlantic*. Howells was right on both counts, but the incident brought attention to a cultural division. In the boom and bust climate of the West that had nurtured Sam, whenever anyone took himself seriously, his friends were sure to deflate his ego with practical jokes or good-natured kidding. Not so in the East. Reputation was everything. You did not joke about it, not even if you were Mark Twain.

Years later, with all remorse behind him, Sam reread the speech and found it "just as good as it can be. It is smart; it is saturated with humor. There isn't a suggestion of coarseness or vulgarity in it anywhere."[2]

Susy and Clara grew more and more appreciative of Sam's stories. They challenged him with any subject to see what kind of yarn he could make of it. He was never beaten at this game, but eventually, when he wanted to work, he had to climb to the billiard room to get away from the girls. There, if not writing, he could at least improve his skill with the cue. On Friday evenings he regularly asked friends to come play the game. He was rarely beaten at this, either.

Sam was not a good businessman. He thought he was and for years was able to ignore any evidence that suggested otherwise. He lost money in speculations again and again. He lost thousands of dollars in a new steam generator that was supposed to cut fuel consumption by 95 percent. It didn't. He put thirty-two thousand dollars into a pulley that was supposed to make cargo hauling more efficient. It didn't. He invested twenty-five thousand dollars in a system that would make telegraphy more efficient. It didn't. After losing his investments in a watch company and then an insurance company, he turned cautious and refused to put anything into Alexander Graham Bell's telephone, thereby missing a fortune.

Thanks to Bliss's insistence on another Mark Twain travel book, Sam decided to take his family to Europe. He and Livy hired a German nurse to teach the whole family German, and they persuaded Clara Spaulding, who had been with them in England, to go to Europe with them.

They sailed on April 11, 1878.

17

A Tramp Abroad

Man is the Only Animal that Blushes. Or needs to.

In Germany, Sam settled his family in Heidelberg, a famous university town. The view from their peaceful hotel included a castle, a forested hillside, the Neckar River, and the distant Rhine Valley. The silence was broken only by singing birds.

Sam also rented a room in a cottage where he could work on notes for the travel book which would be called *A Tramp Abroad*. He also continued to study German and he wrote many letters. By mail, he and Twichell planned a summer walking tour in the Swiss Alps.

To Howells he wrote:

Our bedroom has two great glass bird-cages (inclosed balconies) one looking toward the Rhine Valley and sunset, and the other looking up the Neckar cul-de-sac, and naturally we spend nearly all our time in these. . . . We have tables and

The Reverend Joseph Twichell

chairs in them; we do our reading, writing, studying, smoking, and suppering in them.

They all continued to study German. Rosa, the German nursemaid, spoke to the children only in German, and Livy memorized a German sentence each evening. Sam despaired of ever mastering the language, and marveled that most of the Europeans he met could speak several languages fluently.

While Livy and Clara Spaulding shopped, visited art galleries, or went to the opera for their recreation, Sam preferred long walks or train excursions, activities restricted for Livy by her frail health.

Sam's Alpine holiday with Twichell began on August 1, 1878. They sometimes stayed under cover on rainy days and Sam sometimes took a carriage when troubled with rheumatism, but a day rarely passed without some walking. Their pace was slow. Sam stopped often to take notes. They enjoyed each other's company to the fullest. They collected flowers and talked to the natives. Sam once tried to converse with a stray lamb.

During the evenings in village inns, other guests gathered at the fire to hear Sam talk. No one knew he was Mark Twain except for one young man who was so enthusiastic Twichell had to reveal Sam's identity.

Sam collected further "evidence" of mental telegraphy. Several times he or Twichell would say something that echoed exactly the other's unvoiced thought. One evening, after Twichell saw the book Sam was reading, he mentioned his favorite passage. It happened to be the exact passage Sam had just finished reading.

On the trail one day, after Twichell spoke at length of a friend he knew, they rounded a corner to meet the friend face-to-face. Twichell had no idea the man was also vacationing in the Alps.

Twichell's appreciation of his companion increased with each day. "He has coarse spots in him," the preacher said in a letter home,

> but I never knew a person so finely regardful of the feelings of others in some ways. He hates to pass another person walking, and will practice some subterfuge to take off what he feels is the discourtesy of it. . . . His sensitive regard for others

extends to animals. When we are driving his concern is all about the horse. He can't bear to see the whip used, or to see the horse pull hard. . . .

And later: "Mark is splendid to walk with amid such grand scenery, for he talks so well about it, has such a power of strong, picturesque expression. I wish you might have heard him today. His vigorous speech nearly did justice to the things we saw."[1]

They talked at first on all subjects, but after Sam said he doubted that the Bible had divine inspiration, they agreed not to discuss religion.

Livy waited with the children at Lausanne, Switzerland, and there the men ended their walk. Twichell returned to Hartford, and Sam took his family to Italy. In Venice, Florence, and Rome, the ladies visited galleries almost daily, but Sam was never an art enthusiast.

"Livy and Clara are having a royal time worshipping the old masters," he wrote Twichell, "and I as good a time gritting my ineffectual teeth over them."

Still gathering material for his book, Sam took his family to Munich, Germany, to begin what became a miserable winter. They were tired. It was cold. Sam had trouble working. They tried Paris in February, but it was still cold. Sam suffered. "France," he wrote, "has neither winter, nor summer, nor morals. Apart from these drawbacks it is a fine country."[2]

The American author and Sam's friend Thomas Aldrich was vacationing in Paris with his family and lifted Sam's spirits. His old interest in Joan of Arc returned. He began reading French history and visiting historical sites.

Bad weather continued into the summer as Sam and his family visited Belgium, Holland, and then England. It was still stormy, but friends in London welcomed them warmly. They attended many parties and met many people, including fellow Americans Henry James, the novelist, and James Abbott McNeill Whistler, the artist. It was fun, but Sam and Livy by now were eager to get home. They sailed in late August.

The trip had broadened their views. Livy particularly came home more informed about other creeds and cultures. She was not as likely now to object to some of Sam's strange notions. Sam worked hard on the travel book, but Hartford's social life, as lively as ever, distracted him.

The girls staged charades and plays with the Twichell and Warner children. Sam invented skits, helped with costumes, and sometimes played a role in their production. To the delight of their guests, he also played the piano and sang riverboat songs or spirituals he had learned at the Quarles farm.

Sam went to Chicago in November to participate in a reception for General Ulysses S. Grant, who had just returned from an around-the-world journey. Although Sam's speech came at the end of a long evening, it left everyone laughing, and he and Grant launched a friendship that would continue until the general's death.

Back in Hartford for the winter of 1879–1880, Sam worked on *The Prince and the Pauper*. Because he read aloud each evening what he had written during the day, he kept his style clear and simple enough for the girls to understand and enjoy. It became the family's favorite book. By comparison, *A Tramp Abroad* became a drudgery. He was delighted to finish it and give full attention to his prince.

> I take so much pleasure in my story [he told Howells], that I am loath to hurry, not wanting to get it done. . . .
>
> Imagine this fact: I have even fascinated Mrs. Clemens

with this yarn for youth. My stuff generally gets considerable damning with faint praise out of her, but this time it is all the other way. . . . This is no mean triumph, my dear sir.

A Tramp Abroad, with advance sales of twenty-five thousand copies, came off the presses on March 13, 1880. Critics praised it, and a German translation promptly appeared. Sam was very pleased with the reception, but he was never fully satisfied with the book. Somehow, he had failed to recapture the joyful, carefree spirit and the humor of his earlier travel books.

During the spring, when not working on *Prince,* Sam wrote articles and many letters. He wrote Howells almost daily, once just to say that he had nothing to say.

Orion still worried him. Since closing the chicken farm, his brother had been a salesman, miner, journalist, printer, and lawyer. He had attended nearly every church in and around Keokuk at least once and changed political parties three times. Thinking it might give Orion some stability, Sam suggested that his brother write an autobiography. "Simply tell your story to yourself, laying all hideousness utterly bare, reserving nothing. Banish the idea of an audience and all hampering things."

Immediately, Orion dashed off a hundred pages, and sent them to Sam. Sam was impressed enough to forward the first installment to Howells for use in the *Atlantic.* Howells, however, advised against publication, saying Orion's frank story would make readers uncomfortable.

But nothing could stop Orion. He sent Sam new supplements almost daily. Orion's life story continued long after Sam lost interest. In vain, he tried to stop the flow of words from Keokuk. It was one of the few projects Orion saw to completion, and although it was never published, writing it may have been a help to him.

Meanwhile, Sam, who had been sending irregular sums all along, began giving Orion and Mollie an allowance of seventy-five dollars a month. Orion deserved this, Sam said, for advising him to ask half the profit instead of the usual royalties on his books. The new arrangement, begun with *A Tramp Abroad,* put Sam into virtual partnership with Bliss.

Sam and Livy's last child was born at Quarry Farm on July 26, 1880. Jane Lampton Clemens, named after Sam's mother but known almost from her day of birth as "Jean," was a healthy baby and a great source of pride to her sisters.

Sam wrote Twichell, "It is curious to note the change in stock-quotations on the Affection Board brought about by throwing this new security on the market." He said he was now ranked below the two cats. "That is the way it stands now. Mama is become No. 2; I am dropped from No. 4, and am become No. 5. Some time ago it used to be nip and tuck between me and the cats, but after the cats 'developed' I didn't stand any more show."

Bones, the resident dog, was on good terms with Sam, but Sam liked cats far better than dogs. Susy once said, "The difference between papa and mama is, that mama loves morals and papa loves cats."

Sam worked alternately on *Prince* and the story of Huckleberry Finn that he had started four years earlier. He continued to read evening installments about the young prince to his family, but he had too many misgivings to read the Finn story to them.

Again there were interruptions. Sam went to Washington, D.C., once more to urge better copyright laws. It seemed fruitless, but later when Congress began discussing international treaties, copyright entered the discussion.

When General Grant came to Hartford in the fall to cam-

paign for presidential candidate James Garfield, Sam introduced the general to the crowd. Later, Sam and Joe Twichell
called on the general to obtain his support for one of Twichell's
projects, an educational mission in China. Each meeting
strengthened Sam's friendship with the general.

Sam and Livy supported several charities. At Christmas they
distributed baskets to the poor families of Hartford. Sam also
spoke at the local African-American church, and he and Livy
sponsored one black student's college education. Early in 1881
they sent Karl Gerhardt, a promising sculptor, to Paris for two
years of study.

Meanwhile, Sam's involvement in publishing increased.
After Elisha Bliss died in the fall of 1880, Sam and James R.
Osgood became partners. Sam would pay the cost of publishing
The Prince and the Pauper and give Osgood a 7.5 percent com-
mission on sales. The balance would be profit for Sam. With
Howells, Sam made arrangements with Osgood to publish an
anthology of American humor on the same terms. It was a good
arrangement for Sam, but unfortunately, his interest in publishing would distract him from writing.

CHAPTER 18

The Publisher

As to the Adjective: when in doubt, strike it out.

When he met Grant again in the summer of 1881, Sam urged the general to write his memoirs. Now speaking as a publisher, Sam predicted the book would enjoy immense sales, but Grant showed no interest.

Meanwhile, hoping again to thwart pirates, Sam and Osgood signed a contract with a legitimate firm in Canada for publication of *The Prince and the Pauper*. Thus, in December 1881, the book appeared simultaneously in the United States, England, Germany, and Canada.

A handful of critics expected another humorous book and were disappointed, but the majority lauded Mark Twain's first historical novel. A hit with both children and adults, it reflected Sam's compelling social conscience and showed that he could observe humanity with a keen, sometimes merciless eye.

Meanwhile, despite a string of previous bad investments, Sam put forty thousand dollars into the development of an engraving process that was supposed to revolutionize the printing business. It didn't, but he would not be discouraged. His investments in 1881 alone exceeded one hundred thousand dollars, well above his income for the year. To beef up his income, he published *The Stolen White Elephant,* a collection of his recent sketches and stories, which sold well.

In April 1882, after Sam and Osgood decided to publish a book on Sam's Mississippi recollections, they went to St. Louis and boarded the steamer *Gold Dust.* Sam wanted to refresh his memory. He began the trip under an assumed name, but old friends quickly recognized him.

Fortunately the pilothouse gave him the privacy he needed to take notes and enjoy the journey down the big river. Horace Bixby, the pilot whom Sam had not seen for twenty-one years, greeted him and Osgood at New Orleans. They spent a full day visiting a plantation and recalling old times. Joel Chandler Harris, author of the "Uncle Remus" stories, and George Washington Cable, a leading southern novelist, also provided good company and stimulating, literary conversation.

Bixby, now piloting the luxurious *City of Baton Rouge,* took Sam and Osgood upriver to St. Louis. From there, they went to Hannibal where Sam observed, "The romance of boating is gone now. In Hannibal the steam-boat man is no longer god."[1]

Back in Hartford, while working on his Mississippi book, Sam arranged for Charles L. Webster who had married his niece, Annie Moffett, Pamela's daughter, to go to work for Osgood as a New York subscription manager. Smart and industrious, Webster advanced quickly in the publishing business, gaining more and more responsibility.

Early in 1883 Sam's lecture on "What Is Happiness?" caused much discussion among members of Hartford's Monday Evening Club. Most disagreed with his argument that every human action is basically selfish, but Sam developed the theory further over the years and eventually expanded it in a long essay called *What Is Man?*

"The man who is a pessimist before he is forty-eight knows too much; the man who is an optimist after he is forty-eight knows too little."[2] Sam himself was approaching his forty-eighth birthday when he wrote these lines.

During one of his trips to Canada, checking on copyright matters, Sam was invited to stay with Lord Lorne, the governor-general. Lady Lorne was Queen Victoria's daughter, and even though Sam had long opposed royalty and aristocracy as undemocratic, he felt honored by the attention and lavish hospitality.

Life on the Mississippi came out in May 1883. American and European critics praised it, but it was such a costly edition that profits were small.

The river trip, however, had revived his interest in the unfinished story of Huck Finn, and by August 1883, at Quarry Farm, it had his full attention. He worked six days a week, and if Livy didn't stop him, he worked Sundays as well.

The story of Huck and Jim was all but finished when he returned to Hartford in the fall, but Sam put it aside to collaborate on a play with Howells. They had great fun. The play turned into a farcical revival of the irrepressible Colonel Sellers. The authors had Sellers invent a fire extinguisher and a pair of wings that allowed him to flit across the stage like a butterfly.

Sam and Howells sustained their enthusiasm until a few hours before the Hartford premiere. Then Howells abruptly lost faith and withdrew, assigning all his interest to Sam, and after a few small-town trials of the play, Sam himself lost interest.

The experience, however, led to other plays. In the space of just a few weeks, he dramatized *The Adventures of Tom Sawyer* and *The Prince and the Pauper.* He began writing a drama set in

Oliver Cromwell's England and worked on a Sandwich Islands story which he thought could be turned into a play. These and many other manuscripts were not published.

> Sometimes, my feelings are so hot that I have to take the pen and put them on paper to keep them from setting me afire inside; then all that ink and labor are wasted because I can't print the result. I have just finished an article of this kind, and it satisfies me entirely. It does my weather-beaten soul good to read it, and admire the trouble it would make for me and my family. I will leave it behind and utter it from the grave. There is free speech there, and no harm to the family.[3]

He still found time for fun and invention. In the spring of 1884, with much laughter, Sam and Twichell tried to master the high-wheeled bicycle that had just come on the market. A friend observed that Sam found more ways to fall off than the inventor of the machine ever imagined. Unfortunately, by the time the low-wheeled "safety" bicycle came on the market, Sam had lost interest in cycling in any form.

Southern novelist George Washington Cable, whom Sam had met in New Orleans, was now a resident of Hartford. For an April Fools' Day prank, Cable had friends and neighbors write for Mark Twain's autograph. Letters arrived in bundles, and although puzzled, Sam was fooled at first. Not until some asked for signatures by the yard or by the pound and even for his name on a blank check, did Sam come to his senses. He was pleased just the same by the trouble Cable and his friends had taken to tease him.

Annie's husband Charles Webster, meanwhile, had become manager of the publishing company, leaving Osgood free to run the production end of the business and relieving Sam of many

This bust by Karl Gerhardt was photographed as the frontispiece for the 1884 edition of Adventures of Huckleberry Finn.

business worries. By the time *Adventures of Huckleberry Finn* was ready for publication, Sam and Webster had formed their own firm. Charles L. Webster & Company would be a source of great satisfaction and great trouble.

One of Webster's talents was his ability to work with Sam, whose quick temper and impulsive spirit often made him a difficult partner. Sam repeatedly said, for instance, that he did not want to be bothered with details, but Webster soon learned that Sam would rage if bypassed on even the smallest decision.

Reading proof sheets always taxed Sam's patience. He once told Howells that printing mistakes were enough to "make a man swear his teeth loose." To Webster, Sam wrote that one of the proofreaders "is an idiot; and not only an idiot, but blind, and not only blind, but partly dead."

Soon after the sculptor Karl Gerhardt came back from study in Paris, he made a portrait bust of Sam. Everyone at Quarry Farm was delighted with the result, and Sam had a photo taken of it to use for the frontispiece in *Huck Finn*. Meanwhile, during that summer of 1884, he gave most of his attention to proofs for the book. Livy and the children, particularly Susy, helped, and Sam was delighted with their approval.

The presidential campaign of 1884 was bitter. The Republicans had nominated James G. Blaine, but many liberal members of the party, including Sam and Twichell, thought the man unworthy of the office. Republicans opposed to Blaine were called mugwumps. As a mugwump, Sam campaigned for Grover Cleveland, the Democratic candidate who won the election. Feelings ran so high that Twichell's congregation very nearly dismissed him, and Sam's friendship with Howells, a Blaine man, cooled.

❧ CHAPTER **19**

Grant's Memoirs

By trying we can easily endure adversity. Another man's, I mean.

Sam and George Washington Cable decided to team up on the lecture circuit. Although he had sworn never to lecture again, they would read, thereby avoiding the need to memorize a speech, and Cable would keep Sam from being lonely. On top of everything, Sam needed money to keep the publishing business going and cover losses from his bad investments.

Sam and Cable made an odd pair. Cable didn't smoke or swear, and when he began reading aloud from the Bible in their hotel room after each show, Sam protested so strongly that Cable read thereafter to himself.

On Sundays, while Sam stayed in bed all day reading and smoking, Cable went to church, sometimes to preach, and went to Bible school, often to give the lesson.

Despite their differences, they remained friends, and their show was a success.

They usually opened with Cable reading one of his stories or a selection from some other author. Then Sam would read a piece. Cable would then follow with three selections, and Sam would conclude with three of his, usually including the not-yet-published "King Sollermun" chapter from *Adventures of Huckleberry Finn.*

Always the master showman, Sam drew praise from Howells who wrote after seeing a performance, "You simply straddled down to the footlights and took that house up in the hollow of your hand and tickled it."[1] Sam sometimes wondered whether by playing the buffoon, he was not demeaning himself and undermining his reputation as a serious author.

In November 1884, when he learned that General Grant was negotiating with a publisher for his memoirs, Sam made a quick visit to Grant to remind him that he, Sam, had suggested the memoirs three years previously. Grant eventually signed a contract with Charles L. Webster & Company to publish the book.

Work on these memoirs was well under way when Sam went to Hartford for the Christmas holidays. Livy and the children had prepared a surprise—an elaborate, full-costumed production of *The Prince and the Pauper.* Sam was enchanted. So too were friends and neighbors. The performances had to be repeated again and again, and to his delight, Sam was allowed to play the role of Miles Hendon, rescuer and benefactor of the little prince.

Early in 1885, on the lecture tour again, Cable was surprised to hear Sam confess that he had never read Sir Thomas Malory's *Morte d'Arthur.* Cable promptly bought a copy of the famous legend for Sam. The timing could not have been more apt.

Sam hungered for history and myth, and the story of King Arthur and the knights of the Round Table seemed to put him under a spell. Charmed and excited, he repeatedly compared the medieval England of Arthur's day with the present. He began filling his notebook with ideas.

> . . . No pockets in armor. No way to manage certain require-
> ments of nature. Can't scratch. Cold in the head—can't
> blow—Can't get a handkerchief, can't use iron sleeve. Iron
> gets red hot in the sun—leaks in the rain, gets white with frost
> & freezes me solid in winter. Suffer from lice & fleas. Makes
> disagreeable clatter when I enter church. Can't dress or
> undress myself. Always struck by lightening. Fall down, can't
> get up.[2]

He soon began working on what would become *A Connecticut Yankee in King Arthur's Court.*

In Keokuk for a lecture, Sam enjoyed a happy reunion with Orion, Mollie, and his mother, who was now staying with them. After attending the reading, Jane Clemens, at eighty-one, danced a few steps just to prove she still could. Sam was delighted to see how spry and spirited she was.

By the time Sam returned to Hartford early in 1885, *Huck Finn,* with advance sales of some forty thousand copies, was being delivered to subscribers. There was immediate controversy. Several libraries banned the book because Huck sometimes stole and occasionally lied to protect his friends. The librarians concluded that the book was immoral.

Many saw *Huck Finn* as a protest against prejudice and exploitation of the poor. When Huck decides to risk damnation rather than turn Jim in as a runaway slave, the boy becomes a classical hero, echoing the American conscience. In *Huck Finn,* Mark Twain not only reminded the nation what the war between the states had been about, but he also declared what his country should become.

Huckleberry Finn as pictured by E. W. Kemble, the book's first illustrator

Readers who expected a sequel to *Tom Sawyer* with more boyhood memories were disappointed. *Huck Finn,* though remarkably funny and entertaining, was a serious book. In dealing with slavery and racial prejudice, after all, Mark Twain came to grips with issues that had almost destroyed the nation. The book also explored the old conflict between freedom and responsibility. Even the carefree Huck cannot escape responsibility.

Some scholars recently have claimed that Sam patterned Huck's language after that of a black boy he listened to before writing the book, but it seems just as likely that Sam drew from the speech patterns he learned during his early days among freemen and slaves in the culture that nourished him.

On February 26, 1885, Sam visited Grant and was shocked to find him suffering from cancer of the tongue. In pain, and seriously weakened by the illness, Grant just the same promised to go ahead with his memoirs.

His endeavor made news. Reporters were startled when Sam predicted 250,000 in advance orders. No book had ever reached that figure, but as it turned out, Sam's prediction came true.

Despite his illness, Grant's memory remained remarkably accurate, and by heroic effort, he retained enough energy to write almost daily. When it became too difficult, he dictated his story to a secretary. Sometimes Grant dictated ten thousand words in one sitting.

Sam often visited Grant, to praise what had been written and encourage the general to continue. The cancer spread. Doctors said he might not live more than two or three weeks, but Grant proved them wrong and continued working.

During one visit, when reading the manuscript, Sam discovered that he had almost been captured by Grant back in 1861.

"He surprised an enemy camp near Florida, Missouri, on Salt River which I had been occupying a day or two before," Sam recalled. "How near he came to playing the devil with his future publisher!"[3]

Grant's project encouraged Sam to write about his own war experiences. "The Private History of a Campaign That Failed" was published in the December 1885 issue of *Century* magazine. Grant's efforts, it seems, also inspired Sam to begin dictating an autobiography. Dictating, however, made him uncomfortable, and although he would again begin dictating his autobiography in later life, he was too busy with the publishing business at this time to give his life story further thought.

On June 28, after losing the ability to speak, Grant asked for Sam's help. Several days were needed for revisions. Grant wrote down suggested changes. This process continued more or less steadily until July 19 when General Grant declared the work finished. He died five days later. By then the manuscript was in the hands of the printers.

On November 30, 1885, with the help of friends and hundreds of fans, Sam marked his fiftieth birthday. The Hartford house was deluged with congratulatory letters. Oliver Wendell Holmes even wrote a poem for the occasion.

The summer before, thirteen-year-old Susy Clemens had begun keeping a journal. At Quarry Farm she wrote:

We are a very happy family! We consist of papa, mama, Jean, Clara and me. It is papa I am writing about, and I shall have no trouble in not knowing what to say about him, as he is a very striking character. Papa's appearance has been described many times, but very incorrectly; he has beautiful curly grey hair, not any too thick or any too long, just right; a Roman nose, which greatly improves the beauty of his features, kind

Olivia, Clara, Jean, Susy, and the dog "Hash" gather on a gazebo while Sam struggles with one of his cheap cigars.

blue eyes, a small moustache, he has a wonderfully shaped head, and profile, he has a very good figure. In short he is an extraordinarily fine looking man. All his features are perfect, except that he hasn't extraordinary teeth. His complexion is very fair, and he doesn't wear a beard.

He is a very good man, and a very funny one; he has got a temper but we all of us have in this family. He is the loveliest man I ever saw, or ever hope to see, and oh so absent-minded![4]

Sam was pleased and perhaps a little proud. A success by any measure, he had a happy, loving family, a comfortable home, and a lucrative profession. His books continued to sell briskly. Mark Twain was a name known around the world. And he stood to receive more fame soon as a publisher.

The first volume of *The Personal Memoirs of U. S. Grant* was published on December 1, 1885. Nearly three months later, Webster delivered a royalty check to Grant's widow for two hundred thousand dollars, the largest royalty check written in the history of publishing. The second volume was published in March 1886 and other substantial checks followed. It was an unheard-of success.

Ironically, the success put Sam and Webster on the road to failure. They overspent. They hired too many people. The initial triumph made them expect big profits from every venture. It was not to be. Biographies of other Civil War heroes failed to meet expectations. Biographies of Pope Leo XII and Henry Ward Beecher were also disappointing.

Sam remained optimistic and difficult. When Howells and another man turned in a collaboration on *Mark Twain's Library of Humor,* Sam revised it so much that he upset everyone involved. He bombarded Webster with new ideas. When he visited the office, he ordered so many changes in the operation that the staff lost time setting things right again.

Overworked and worried, Webster's health began to fail. His assistant Fred J. Hall, dedicated but less experienced, took over most chores, but Sam had to assume more responsibility.

Remarkably, Sam still found time to write and pursue a variety of interests. He began doing exercises to improve his memory, and when a Hartford woman preached "mind cure" as a remedy for colds, stomachaches, and scores of other ailments,

Sam enthusiastically adopted the methods and soon had everyone in his household "thinking away" their minor illnesses.

There were still many visitors. Sam made friends with novelist Robert Louis Stevenson and with Charles Dickens's son and his family. Once after a hilarious evening in Sam's company, English poet and critic Matthew Arnold asked if Mark Twain were ever serious. One of Sam's friends answered that Mark Twain was the most serious man in the world.

Meanwhile, Sam and Livy launched the Browning Club, which met regularly in Hartford to read and discuss the poems of Robert Browning. Later when actor Edwin Booth organized the Players Club in New York, Sam was among the first invited to join, and from then on, during business trips to the city, he usually stayed in the club's comfortable bachelor dwelling at 16 Gramercy Park.

In June 1888 Yale University conferred an honorary Master of Arts degree on Mark Twain. Although unable to attend the ceremony, he wrote a humorous directive befitting his new role of college dignitary. He ordered the Greek professor to stop writing that language because the spelling was so difficult, told the mathematics professor to simplify the system so more people could understand it, and advised the university astronomer to stop looking at comets and asteroids because there was already plenty of information on such things.

Sam by now had begun to borrow money from Livy's inheritance to keep his publishing business afloat and to support his various speculations. His latest interest was in a typesetting machine that he believed would revolutionize the printing industry and make him rich beyond measure. It didn't.

ℰ CHAPTER 20

The Typesetter

There are two times in a man's life when he should not speculate:
when he can't afford it, and when he can.

A friend had introduced Sam to James W. Paige in 1880. Sam liked the inventor at once. He was a small, neat man with bright eyes, and he worked with great confidence and intensity on a machine that promised to set type faster, more accurately, and cheaper than human hands.

The contraption still needed work, but Sam put up two thousand dollars to allow Paige to finish the job. They talked about forming a company to market the machine as soon as it was perfected.

"I was always taking little chances like that, and almost always losing by it, too,"[1] Sam recalled.

This, however, was no little chance. Sam, it turned out, had become involved with a perfectionist. When he returned to see Paige's invention several weeks later, it was actually setting type. Sam was satisfied, but Paige was not. The machine, he

James W. Paige's ruinous typesetting machine

explained, could not yet justify a line of type. With more time and money, however, he could make it insert the necessary spaces between letters so that the margins were equal, or justified, on both sides of the type column.

As it was, the machine with a man hired to insert spaces would probably have been a commercial success, but Paige would not hear of it.

Sam had no formal commitment with Paige until 1886 when he put up several thousand dollars more and signed a contract promising to promote the machines when they went on the market. Although warned that the venture would bankrupt him, and that other inventors were working on simpler, less expensive machines, Sam's faith was unshaken. As he gave Paige more and more money, Sam claimed that the typesetter would soon make him rich.

Despite increasing financial worries, Sam worked steadily on

A Connecticut Yankee in King Arthur's Court. When he left the isolation of Quarry Farm in the fall of 1888, however, he was too worried to write regularly. Even after he borrowed a room from Twichell to use as an office, Sam remained distracted.

The summer of 1889 was a sad one. Theodore Crane, Livy and Sam's beloved brother-in-law, died, and his generous, warm companionship was missed by all. With Crane gone, Sam and his family did not spend much time at Quarry Farm again until the summer of 1895.

Susy Clemens managed to write a play that summer and soon after the family returned to Hartford, it was produced in the Clemens home. Sam proudly insisted on several repeat performances. Meanwhile, Elsie Leslie, who was starring in a commercial production of *The Prince and the Pauper,* visited the Clemens children frequently.

Sam hoped when he sent the manuscript to the printers that *A Connecticut Yankee in King Arthur's Court* would solve his financial ills. It had been five years since *Huck Finn* appeared, and Sam believed the public was ready for what he mistakenly believed would be his final book. "It's my swan song, my retirement from literature permanently," he told Howells. "Well, my book is finished—let it go, but if it were only to write over again there wouldn't be so many things left out. They burn in me; they keep multiplying and multiplying, but now they can't ever be said; and besides they would require a library—and a pen warmed in hell."

Even so, Sam had loaded the book with so much personal philosophy that it distracted from his story. In setting his own democratic and socialistic ideals against the tyranny of medieval kings, he had injected a sermon into an imaginative adventure. There were plenty of humor and a host of entertaining characters, but much of the book was meant to be taken seriously.

Americans generally praised the book. Howells thought it one of Sam's best. Many English readers and critics, however, were outraged. Mark Twain, it seemed, had attacked their history, their proud traditions, and even their system of government. By taking his hero back in time to early England, Mark Twain had made their ancestors appear cruel and stupid, and to suggest that a humble American mechanic from the nineteenth century could run their country better than King Arthur himself was nothing more than a vulgar insult. One English critic declared that Mark Twain's books, after all, were "not for the cultivated class."

Sam's reaction was typical. In a letter to a friend, he said he had never hoped to reach "the cultivated class" and "never had any ambitions in that direction, but always hunted for bigger game—the masses."[2]

When his English publishers wanted to revise the book to make it more palatable to English sensitivities, Sam refused, saying:

> This is important for the reason that the book was not written for America; it was written for England. So many Englishmen have done their sincerest best to teach us something for our betterment that it seems to me high time that some of us should substantially recognize the good intent by trying to pry up the English nation to a little higher level of manhood in turn.

Unfortunately, production costs had been so high that the book, despite good sales, did not return big profits. Sam went to work on the manuscript for a book he planned to call *Huck Finn and Tom Sawyer Among the Indians*. After nine chapters, however, he gave up on the project.

Sam's troubles multiplied. Paige needed more money. The

publishing firm was on a steep decline. Sam's mother, now eighty-seven, was in failing health, and Sam himself had developed rheumatism in his right arm and shoulder. It pained him to write.

Sam and Livy had hoped to take the family to Europe in the summer of 1890, but they simply could not afford it. Instead they took a cabin at Onteora Park, a retreat for intellectuals near Tannersville in the Catskill Mountains.

The cabins lay clustered around a rustic country inn that served as a gathering place for artists and writers and their families. They played cards, swapped stories, and to the delight of Sam and his girls, put on innumerable pantomimes and charades.

Carroll Beckwith, a fellow camp resident, painted Sam's portrait, but Sam had to interrupt his holiday frequently to tend to financial problems in New York. In August he rushed to Keokuk to see his mother. She seemed near death when he arrived, but his visit apparently helped her rally. Sam returned to his family much relieved.

On October 27, 1890, however, after the Clemenses had returned to Hartford, Jane Lampton Clemens died. She was buried in Hannibal beside the grave of John Marshall Clemens who had died forty-three years earlier.

Sam had barely returned from the funeral when Livy's mother died in Elmira. Back at Hartford, the big house seemed empty and depressing. Jean was sick and Susy had left for her first year at Bryn Mawr.

Faith in Paige blunted Sam's judgment. He turned down the chance to trade Paige's patents for a half interest in the Mergenthaler Linotype machine, then being developed. A few years later, the Linotype was in worldwide use.

Paige, meanwhile, had discarded his first design in favor of a complex contraption with twenty thousand precision-made, moving parts. Only a highly skilled mechanic could keep the machine running. Sam put up more money, money that might have been used to rescue the publishing business.

For a few hours on January 5, 1889, the Paige machine came to life, setting and justifying line after line of type without a hitch. Sam was ecstatic.

"This is the first time in the history of the world that this amazing thing has ever been done," Sam wrote in his notebook. In a letter to Orion he declared, "All the other wonderful inventions of the human brain sink pretty nearly into commonplaces contrasted with this awful mechanical miracle."

Paige was not satisfied. Because it occasionally broke the type, he took the machine apart. He had it together and working again in February, but then took it apart again. He wanted to make some changes. Several months passed before the machine ran again.

Sam tried early in 1890 to raise two million dollars for a stock company that would produce and sell the machine. He enlisted Joe Goodman's help in raising the money, but the machine did not cooperate. Potential investors were not interested in a machine that was regularly being dismantled for improvements.

Sam by now had sunk some $190,000 into the typesetter and he had borrowed more money to keep the publishing business afloat.

In describing his plight to a friend, Sam recalled having done everything from newspaper reporting to piloting, to mining, to printing, to writing. "I have been an author for 20 years and an ass for 55. . . ."

CHAPTER 21

Bankruptcy

October. This is one of the particularly dangerous months to speculate in stocks in. The others are July, January, September, April, November, May, March, June, December, August, and February.

Sam thought writing offered his best chance for raising quick money. He polished up two unpublished articles and sold them to *Harper's Magazine* and then went to work on a novel about Colonel Sellers, building on the plot he and Howells had developed for their unsuccessful play.

The hero became an English lord who renounces title and property to come to America to practice progressive political ideas.

In February 1891, when rheumatism made writing painful, Sam tried a dictating machine that recorded his words on a wax cylinder. It was difficult to adjust to this method, and the novel itself presented problems. It was part wildly funny farce and part serious political sermon.

Charles L. Webster died on April 26, 1891. He had been ill for a long time, but his death depressed Sam immensely. Despite his grief, he continued his work and by May, had written enough to sell serial rights to the story in both England and America. He called it *An American Claimant.* It brought in twelve thousand dollars.

Meanwhile, they all needed a rest. Livy, who also had rheumatism, had developed a weak heart. Susy had returned from Bryn Mawr in poor health. Sam needed something to take his mind off his worries, so when a publisher offered him six thousand dollars for six letters from Europe, the Clemens family decided to travel. To economize, they closed the Hartford house. Livy's sister, Susan Crane, now a widow, and Katie Leary, the family nursemaid, would travel with them.

They sailed on June 6, 1891, and soon found themselves in Bayreuth, Germany, in time for the famous Wagner Festival where Sam confessed that his attendance at a Wagnerian opera made him feel "like a heretic in heaven."[1]

Rheumatism in his arms still made writing difficult, but readers loved his letters. He wrote from Nuremberg and Heidelberg in Germany before moving to Switzerland.

For ten days in September he drifted with a guide down the Rhône River in a small boat. Then he took his family to Berlin for the winter. The United States minister there was an old friend, and he kept Sam and his family busy attending parties and receptions. Mark Twain was often the main attraction at these parties. But Susy, now a pretty and vivacious nineteen, received her share of dazzling attention.

Sam had many German fans and he set them howling one evening with a lecture in which he used an original and outrageous mixture of German and English. The lecture, however, was held in a hot, crowded hall, and after coming home through the winter chill, Sam fell ill with pneumonia. Bedridden for nearly a month, he eventually recovered enough to receive visitors and finish his final European letter.

Soon after a banquet given in his honor by Emperor William II, Sam and Livy sought warmer weather in the south of France. Susan Crane, Katie Leary, and the children remained in Berlin. They would join their parents later in Rome.

From Rome they went to Florence and liked it so much that they rented the Villa Viviani outside the city for use during the following winter. Then they returned to Germany. Sam settled his family at Bad Nauheim for the summer before sailing on business to America.

Adding to his financial woes was the general economic depression of 1892. Sam wanted to sell his company's rights to *The Library of American Literature,* but he could not find a buyer. The depression had also dampened sales of *The American Claimant.*

Surprisingly, news on the typesetter seemed good. Paige had persuaded some investors to start building a factory. With this encouraging development, Sam, who had planned to sell his interest in the typesetter, now decided against it and once again missed a chance to recover his losses.

He returned to Europe in better spirits and better health than he had enjoyed for many months. The pain in his arm had eased enough for him to write again daily. He worked on several articles and stories and began two book-length manuscripts—*Tom Sawyer Abroad* and *Those Extraordinary Twins.*

The Twichells visited the Clemens family in Germany, and while Sam and Joe were walking in Homburg one morning, they met the Prince of Wales, later England's Edward VII. The prince, a Mark Twain fan, invited the two men to dine with him.

Sam took his family to Florence in September. The Villa Viviani, on a hill surrounded by vineyards and olive trees, gave them a distant view of Florence and a wonderful sense of peace. The old building, with yellow walls and green shutters, had a shaded garden and sunny terrace.

In the evening the family usually gathered on the terrace to watch the sunset. Their numbers were reduced by now. Susan Crane had returned to America, and Clara had gone to Berlin to study the piano.

The comfortable terrace and garden made it possible for Sam to work outside almost every day. Here he finished *Tom Sawyer Abroad* and gave full attention to *Those Extraordinary Twins,* which he later renamed *The Tragedy of Pudd'nhead Wilson.* He also wrote "The 1,000,000 Pound Bank Note," one of his best short stories, and began planning a book about Joan of Arc.

Forty years had passed since chance brought one page of her story to his attention, but he had not forgotten her. When he began at last to write about Joan of Arc, he saw her history as his most serious undertaking.

After some false starts, the book began to move quickly. The research slowed him for he had to translate some material from French. Then he wrote some one hundred thousand words in six weeks. As in the past, he thought for a time of publishing the book anonymously so that it would be taken seriously.

In March 1893, with the book about half-finished, bad financial news forced him once again to return to America. The depression had deepened, but as soon as he arrived in New York in early April, his friends rallied to cheer him. Howells, whom he had not seen for two years, called at his hotel. Later, Sam and his friends dined with English author Rudyard Kipling. The next night, Sam found himself dining with financier Andrew Carnegie. Carnegie, it turned out, was not interested in backing the Paige typesetting machine. No one was.

Sam spent eleven days in Chicago, confined most of that time to his hotel room with a cold. Paige said construction of fifty machines had begun and profits could be expected within a year.

"What a talker he is!" Sam noted. "He could persuade a fish to come out and walk with him. When he is present I always believe him; I can't help it."[2]

Just the same, Sam returned to Europe more optimistic than before. He could not, however, ignore reality. His publishing business faced ruin and the depression made it impossible to borrow money to save it. Sam asked the family to do everything possible to reduce household expenses. He was too worried to write steadily.

They closed the villa in June and went to Munich, Germany, where Clara joined them. The news from home grew worse. Paige reported that ten, rather than fifty, machines would be built and it was not certain buyers could be found. Sam, meanwhile, feared that he might lose the royalties to his books if Charles L. Webster & Company failed. In August he once again sailed for America. This time he would see things through to the sad end.

Although he could afford to go out very little, he was fortunate one night to meet Henry Rogers, one of the principal owners of the Standard Oil Company. With his excellent business sense and generous nature, Rogers soon took Sam's business troubles in hand.

Rogers's calm confidence restored Sam's spirits, and things began to happen. Within a few weeks, he helped negotiate the sale of *The Library of American Literature* for fifty thousand dollars, thus covering two of Sam's most pressing debts. Rogers also investigated the typesetting venture to see what could be salvaged. And best of all, he persuaded Sam to stop worrying.

Sam went out in public once again. He gave a charity lecture in Boston, was guest of honor at the Lotos Club in New

*Sam and Henry H. Rogers are shown together in 1908, long after Sam's
financial disasters were behind them.*

York, and attended several private parties where his presence
was always appreciated. He and Rogers became close friends.
Sam's energy again seemed limitless. One evening, after seeing
a boxing match in Madison Square Garden, he went to a party
and danced until four thirty in the morning. After another long
evening, Rogers asked Sam if he knew what it meant to be
tired. "I wish I did,"[3] he replied.

Sam wrote cheerful letters to Livy and the children describing his adventures. He had met the electrical genius Nikola Tesla, the celebrity journalist Richard Harding Davis, and the famous painter William H. Chase. Sam also wrote that he would soon have good financial news.

Although Rogers did negotiate a new contract with Paige, relieving Sam of some obligations, the outlook remained bleak. Just the same, Sam managed to write. Early in 1894 he completed an essay for the *North American Review* on James Fenimore Cooper's "Literary Offenses," an essay that remains a landmark in caustic literary criticism.

In March both Livy and Susy fell ill, and a concerned Sam took a trip to Europe to make sure they were comfortable. He stayed with them for three weeks before hurrying back to New York.

Rogers had bad news. Charles L. Webster & Company must declare bankruptcy. The legal step was taken on April 18, 1894. Rogers presided at a meeting of creditors and persuaded most of them to wait for their payment.

When a few of the creditors insisted on foreclosure, Rogers protected Sam's main interests by saying Olivia Clemens had first claim on copyrights and outright ownership of the house in Hartford. The meeting concluded with Sam owing seventy thousand dollars. Although the creditors agreed to accept fifty cents on the dollar, Sam vowed to pay everyone in full. Then he fell ill.

Rogers took Sam home where Mrs. Rogers and her family fussed over him and nursed him slowly back to health, back to a point where he could begin to face the future.

22

Around the World

Grief can take care of itself; but to get the full value of joy you must have someone to divide it with.

The failure of Mark Twain's publishing house made front-page news. Waiting for Sam in Europe and not well, Livy suffered grief and shame. To Susan Crane she confessed, "Most of the time I want to lie down and cry. Everything seems to me so impossible. I do not make things go very well, and I feel my life is an absolute and irretrievable failure."[1]

Sam, who was used to public scrutiny, took the events in stride. He wrote Livy cheerfully. "Mr. Rogers is perfectly satisfied that our course was right, absolutely right and wise—cheer up, the best is yet to come."

The experience made Sam appreciate his friends more than ever before. Everyone wanted to help. Financier Andrew Carnegie, his old collaborator Charles Dudley Warner, and several others sent money. Sam returned it all with thanks.

Frank Bliss, now running the American Publishing

Company, eagerly took *The Tragedy of Pudd'nhead Wilson* for publication.

The book today does not get the attention it deserves. Wilson, a struggling attorney, not much respected, in a town very much like Hannibal, collects fingerprints to prove his theory that no two people have the same prints. One of Twain's most delightful characters, Wilson is considered the town crackpot until a dramatic courtroom climax when he is able to use his collection of fingerprints to solve a murder.

Besides being one of America's early mystery novels, the book also had a serious purpose. Mark Twain wanted to demonstrate that environment shaped character far more than did heredity.

Sam returned to Europe in May 1893 and took his family to southern France. There he learned from home that a factory-built, Paige typesetter would be tested by the *Chicago Times-Herald.* Sam's spirits soared. His faith had been justified. He could soon pay all his debts. He might have returned to America at once had he not been warned that tests of the machine would take several weeks.

He worked for about a month on the Joan of Arc story before taking the family to Rouen where, in 1431, the English had tried Joan for sorcery and burned her at the stake.

Susy Clemens was deeply involved in Joan's story by now. Poor health often kept her indoors, but she was never too sick to listen to Sam read or advise him on the story. Sam grew to think of the job as Susy's book.

From Rouen they went to Paris where Susy's health and Livy's spirits improved. Old friends called on them. Sam wrote diligently. Life, it seemed, had returned to normal. But their troubles were not over.

In the fall of 1893, after the machine broke its usual stack of type and suffered breakdowns even its inventor could not explain, the *Times-Herald* rejected the typesetter, and Rogers decided that Paige's marvelous contraption was simply too complex to be practical.

Sam wrote that the news "hit me like a thunder clap. It knocked every rag of sense out of my head." At first he could not accept Rogers's decision but later he wrote, "There's one thing which makes it difficult for me to soberly realize that my ten-year dream is actually dissolved; and that is that it reverses my horoscope. The proverb says 'Born lucky, *always* lucky.'"

Although Sam would one day joke about his other follies, the machine remained a painful memory. When Mergenthaler paid twenty thousand dollars for Paige's patents and assets, it only reminded Sam of the failure. Eventually Paige's machine went on exhibit at Sibley College of Engineering as the costliest piece of machinery for its size ever devised by man and, by the way, as Mark Twain's biggest mistake.

Faced with further economies, Sam and Livy decided to lease the Hartford house. He wrote with renewed energy. Back in Villa Viviani near Florence, Sam finished *The Personal Recollections of Joan of Arc.*

Meanwhile, *The Tragedy of Pudd'nhead Wilson* had been issued to critical acclaim. The book not only established Sam as a pioneer of the mystery novel, it also gave him new stature as a philosopher. Each chapter began with an aphorism supposedly taken from Pudd'nhead Wilson's Calendar. The aphorisms remain highly quotable to this day.

"Let us endeavor so to live that when we come to die even the undertaker will be sorry."

"Training is everything. The peach was once a bitter almond; cauliflower is nothing but cabbage with a college education."

"Nothing so needs reforming as other people's habits."

"Few things are harder to put up with than the annoyance of a good example."

"It was wonderful to find America, but it would have been more wonderful to miss it."

"It is often the case that the man who can't tell a lie thinks he is the best judge of one."

Sam sold serial rights for the Joan of Arc story to *Harper's Magazine* with the understanding that, to make sure it would be taken seriously, it would appear unsigned. Authorship was soon discovered, however, and when Bliss printed the book, it bore Mark Twain's name.

A dispute rose between *Harper's* and Bliss over publishing rights early in 1895, forcing Sam to return to America to set things straight. During this brief trip, he made up his mind to lecture again. As much as he disliked it, lecturing offered the best solution to his financial problems.

He planned his tour on a grand scale. He would go around the world talking and taking notes. When he got home, he would write another travel book. Livy and the two older girls agreed to go with him. This time Sam would not be lonely.

Travel plans were being discussed daily when Sam and his family returned to America in May 1895. Quarry Farm, which they had not seen for many summers, seemed unchanged. The girls, now young ladies, found their playhouse just as they had left it.

They would head west, across North America and then across the Pacific. He would lecture in the United States and Canada, Australia, New Zealand, India, and Africa. It was agreed at first that Jean only would stay behind at Elmira with her aunt, Susan Crane, but at the last minute, Susy, who hated sea voyages, also decided to stay behind. Thus, as the train pulled away from Elmira on July 14, 1895, they had their final

During his world-circling lecture tour, Sam had happy hours at sea to restore his energy and his spirits.

view of Susy, waving farewell with the others on the station platform.

From the start, the tour received so much favorable publicity that its success was assured. In each town, crowds cheered Mark Twain's arrival and packed the houses to hear him read. He was going forth to pay his debts, and all the world, it seemed, wanted to help and encourage him. The money flowed in. From Vancouver, he was able to send home five thousand dollars, the first of many installments against his debt.

He was already tired. He had started with a cold and a carbuncle, a hard growth more persistent and much more painful than a pimple. He had lost weight. Livy, tired herself, fussed and worried over him, but they both enjoyed the attention and praise. An official committee always welcomed them. Fresh flowers adorned every hotel room. Their spirits rose, and then they boarded a ship for a long, restful sea voyage that restored their health and energy.

To Sam's great dismay, a cholera epidemic prevented their landing at Honolulu. He had hoped to renew many old friendships, but the ship sailed on into the sunset.

Except for one stormy day, the passage to Australia was calm. Sam went to work in Sydney, eager and well rested. Full houses greeted him. Although he varied his program, he usually read from *Roughing It, Innocents Abroad,* and either *Tom Sawyer* or *Huck Finn.* Treated as celebrities, Sam, Livy, and Clara attended one party after another. Sam's genuine interest in customs, history, and people made him a popular tourist everywhere.

At the end of September he sent Rogers two thousand dollars, the profits from just two weeks in Australia, but in Melbourne, another carbuncle forced him to rest for a week.

"The dictionary says a carbuncle is a kind of jewel," Sam wrote. "Humor is out of place in a dictionary."[2]

Later, after a doctor said he was on the verge of being a sick man, Sam responded, "I have been on the verge of being an angel all my life, but it's never happened yet."[3]

In New Zealand, where he marked his sixtieth birthday without much enthusiasm, Sam suffered the indignity of yet another carbuncle. Then he caught a cold during the voyage to

Ceylon, now Sri Lanka, but he refused to rest. In India, the pace became hectic, with many hours of uncomfortable travel by train. He performed in Bombay, Beneares, Calcutta, Darjeeling, Lahore, Lucknow, and Delhi. Because lecture halls were small, he often repeated his performance two or three times to satisfy demand.

Sam loved the attention of the Indian and British officials and reveled in the parties given to honor him and his family, but hot weather forced them to leave India in March. They crossed the Indian Ocean to Africa. Calm seas and warm, tropical nights gave Sam the chance to read and sleep. In his contentment, he wished the voyage would never end.

When they arrived in Durban, South Africa, where mail had been held for them, Sam and Livy were puzzled to find no letters from Susy. Livy had grave forebodings. They had been away too long.

Nothing could be done. While Livy and Clara remained in Durban, Sam traveled from city to city on his busy schedule. Then, as now, the country was in political turmoil. A recent rebellion had been suppressed, and Sam soon took sides, urging leniency for the jailed leaders of the rebellion. By the time he left, South African authorities were glad to see the last of Mark Twain.

They sailed for England on July 14. Livy by now was beside herself with worry. They had planned to rent a house near London and have Kate Leary bring Susy and Jean to join them for a long holiday, but when they arrived in England, a letter from home told them that Susy was too sick to travel. Livy and Clara sailed at once for America. Sam rented a little cottage and waited for news.

The public knew nothing of their fears. As far as the rest of the world knew, Mark Twain had returned as conquering hero, having paid his debts with honor.

On August 18, while Livy and Clara were still at sea, Sam received a cable that said, "SUSY WAS PEACEFULLY RELEASED TODAY."

Nothing had prepared him for the shock. Never would he hold his beloved Susy in his arms again. Letters soon told him the full story.

At first Susy had been in good health, practicing her singing regularly until the first weeks of summer. Even after she began feeling listless, she kept practicing. "Mind cure" did not help, and when Katie Leary began helping her get ready to sail to England to join the family, it became clear at once that Susy was seriously ill. The doctor, unable to diagnose the trouble, could only advise rest. Katie Leary and Mrs. Crane opened up the Hartford house and put Susy to bed in her old room. Joe Twichell gave up his summer vacation to help care for the girl.

Susy was delirious and in pain before a doctor finally realized she had meningitis. It was too late. She went blind. She could barely speak. At the end, she put feverish hands on Katie Leary's face and whispered, "Mama."

Again, Sam blamed himself. If he had not invested foolishly, if he had not fallen into debt, if he had not been forced to travel—. In his anguish, he somehow believed he could have prevented Susy's death if he had been with her.

In New York Twichell met Livy and Clara at the dock to tell them the terrible news. He then escorted them to Elmira to see Susy buried.

23

Vienna

In statesmanship get the formalities right,
never mind about the moralities.

Soon after the funeral, Livy, along with Jean, Clara, and Katie Leary, sailed back to England to join Sam. He had given up the cottage and rented a house in a quiet part of London. Only a few friends knew where he and his bereaved family would live.

To the public, he seemed to have vanished, but when a newspaper printed the rumor that his family had abandoned him and that he was laboring alone to repay his debts, he came forward with a denial. Later he wrote to the *New York Herald* to ask that a Mark Twain relief drive be stopped. And finally, when rumors had it that he had died, he told a reporter, "Just say the report of my death has been greatly exaggerated."[1]

In the fall of 1896 he began *Following the Equator*. He found it difficult. All his travel notebooks, all his recollections reminded him of Susy. Sam wrote Twichell saying that he should have praised her more often. "And now she is dead—& I can never tell her."

To Howells he asked, "Will healing ever come, or life have value again? And shall we see Susy? Without doubt! without a *shadow* of doubt if it can furnish opportunity to break our hearts again."

Work sustained him. He sometimes began as early as four A.M. Gradually, outside interests returned. He wrote Rogers asking him to see to the needs of Helen Keller, a blind and deaf woman who was then struggling to complete college.

The Personal Recollections of Joan of Arc was neither a financial nor a critical success. Readers did not expect a scholarly history from Mark Twain. Sam, however, thought it his best work, and eventually, as sales improved, he said his faith had been justified. He still regarded it as Susy's book.

Livy helped edit the travel book. When she insisted that Sam take out "crude" words such as *stench* and *offal,* he protested in one of his many notes, "You are steadily weakening the English tongue, Livy."[2] Despite their differences, and many revisions by Sam, *Following the Equator* finally went to Bliss in May 1897.

With the job behind him, Sam went out more and saw more people. A friend took him to London's Savage Club where the members voted to accept him as an honorary member. He wrote a report for American papers on Queen Victoria's jubilee, celebrating her sixtieth year on the English throne.

Sam then moved his household, which now included Mrs. Crane and Charley Langdon's daughter, Julia, to Switzerland for the summer. He worked on short stories and articles, but spent most of his time and energy reading proofs for the travel book.

On August 18, 1897, the anniversary of Susy's death, Livy

went alone to a hotel room and reread her daughter's letters. Sam wrote a memorial poem.

September found them in Vienna, Austria, where they soon fell under the spell of Europe's gayest society complete with music, dancing, and aristocratic splendor. Clara took piano lessons, Sam and Livy attended innumerable banquets and balls. Already popular, Sam rarely missed a chance to win more fans.

When he spoke to members of the Concordia Club, which numbered some of Europe's best writers, composers, artists, and diplomats, Sam surprised everyone by speaking in German.

A varied and constant parade of visitors at their hotel prompted Livy to write: "Such funny combinations are here sometimes: one duke, several counts, several writers, several barons, two princes, newspaper women, etc. I find so far, without exception, that the high-up aristocracy are simple and cordial and agreeable."[3]

Sam and Livy liked Vienna so much that they stayed on far longer than originally intended. *Following the Equator* went on sale in November and was well received. Although more serious than his previous travel books, Sam again used aphorisms at the start of each chapter.

"Prosperity is the best protector of principle."

"When in doubt, tell the truth."

Jean's health worsened in Vienna. She was an epileptic, and now, after a long period of mild episodes, her seizures grew more frequent and more severe. Meanwhile, the family learned that Orion Clemens, age seventy-two, had died on December 11, 1897. Rogers had better news. Sam's debts had been paid in full and he even came out a few thousand dollars ahead.

With money in the bank, Sam might have invested in a carpet-making machine if Rogers had not dissuaded him. Later, without consulting Rogers, Sam invested five thousand English pounds in a powdered milk process that actually did make money. The company produced Plasmon, a rather tasteless health food. Although most of Sam's friends sampled the stuff without enthusiasm, the British army thought it healthy enough for the troops and eventually became the biggest Plasmon buyer.

With his old energy restored, Sam sometimes wrote eight or nine hours a day and then spent the evening with Livy at a dance or a banquet. His stories, essays, and reviews all became more serious. Rather than having readers laugh, he now preferred that they think.

He protested the Spanish-American War. "When the United States sent word to Spain that the Cuban atrocities must end, she occupied the highest moral position ever taken by a nation since the Almighty made the earth. But when she snatched the Philippines she stained the flag."[4]

Although Sam still believed in "mind cure," he criticized Mary Baker Eddy and her Christian Science Church, saying she was motivated more by love for authority than by the Christian spirit.

After he wrote a controversial article on the conditions of Jews in Europe, he said in a letter to Rogers, "Neither Jew nor Christian will approve of it, but people who are neither Jew nor Christian will, for they are in a condition to know the truth when they see it."

Sam at this time also began his ironic series of letters to Satan. "I have no special regard for Satan, but I can at least claim I have no prejudice against him. It may be that I lean a little his way on account of his not having a fair show."

The tone of the letters would have shocked Livy and the girls, but Sam not only did not show them to anyone, but he also directed that they be published only after his death. The work, published as *Letters from the Earth* (1962), ranks Mark Twain as a leading social satirist.

In the same vein, Sam experimented with several versions of a story about a miracle-working alien who visits Earth in human form. Although his motives are pure, the greed and weaknesses of a small community thwart his good deeds. *The Man That Corrupted Hadleyburg,* a short novel, once again contradicted his reputation as a humorist.

One notebook entry at this time declared, "No man that ever lived has ever done a thing to please God—primarily. It was done to please himself, *then* God next."[5]

He kept abreast of events and was often asked for his opinions in interviews. He sometimes referred to himself as ambassador-at-large for the United States. Indeed, journalists often gave more weight to Mark Twain's opinions than those of government officials.

In response to the Russian czar's call for disarmament, Sam said, "The Tsar is ready to disarm. I am ready to disarm. Collect the others; it should not be much of a task now."[6]

The Austrian emperor Franz Joseph asked Mark Twain to the palace. The party was so friendly and informal that Sam forgot to deliver a speech that he had rehearsed in German. When Sam and his family finally left Vienna in May 1899, a large crowd came to the station to bid them farewell. Their train compartment overflowed with flowers.

They went to London where social invitations again over-whelmed them. Sam was happy to praise Rudyard Kipling at a meeting of the Authors Club, but he and Livy could not enter the social life with much enthusiasm. They were too worried about Jean's epilepsy. In July they took her to an osteopath in Sweden. The man specialized in epilepsy and his treatments seemed to help Jean. Sam was so pleased that he took some of the treatments himself.

They returned to London in October in good spirits. Sam gave so many after-dinner speeches during this period that he found little time to write. He did, however, prepare an introduction to an English edition of *Joan.*

When the editor changed what he had written, Sam vented his rage in a letter.

> It is discouraging to try to penetrate a mind like yours. You ought to get it out & dance on it.
>
> That would take some of the rigidity out of it. And you ought to use it sometimes; that would help. If you had done this every now & then along through life it would not have petrified.

Sam did not mail the letter, but the introduction was restored as he had written it.

℘ CHAPTER 24

Settling Down

It could probably be shown by facts and figures that there is no distinctly native American criminal class except Congress.

Sam and his family now yearned to end what he called "this everlasting exile," but they stayed in England so that Jean could continue her treatments at a London clinic.

Although he and Livy agreed that Susy's spirit made it impossible to live in the Hartford house again, they wanted a permanent home someplace. They had hoped to be back in America before the new century began, but they remained in London through the spring of 1900. Sam wrote about current events.

The Boer War, pitting the English against the Dutch settlers in South Africa, drew some acid from his pen. In a letter to Twichell, he called the war "sordid and criminal." Although a pacifist, he saw the Dutch settlers as the underdogs and the English as oppressors. "I notice that God is on both sides in this war, thus history repeats itself. But I am the only person who has noticed this; everybody here thinks He is playing the game for this side, & for this side only."

In July Sam rented Dollis Hill, a country house surrounded by well-groomed gardens outside of London. The move did not stop the flow of visitors. Sam was particularly comfortable with artists and writers, many of whom also opposed the war.

Sam's only complaint about Dollis Hill was that it was too pleasant to leave, but finally, on October 6, 1900, the Clemens family sailed for America.

Mark Twain's homecoming was a major event. Every newspaper in the country, it seemed, praised his character and his literary genius and described how he had come through debt and tragedy with honor. The joy was tempered with sorrow.

Five days after his return, Sam was called to be a pallbearer at the funeral of Charles Dudley Warner, his old friend and collaborator.

In New York he and Livy moved into a furnished house on West Tenth Street. At once the place became a public attraction. Nearly everyone had to see where Mark Twain lived. Bold fans knocked on the door asking to shake his hand or simply voice their appreciation. Some asked for his autograph.

Sam hired a secretary to answer the door, schedule interviews, and sort through the daily bundles of mail. Jean taught herself to type and take dictation so she could help with her father's correspondence.

Both Sam and Livy were thoroughly tired of parties by now. Just the same, Sam continued to give after-dinner talks. He usually arrived late, however, about the time coffee was being poured. Thus he avoided the tedium of a long banquet. Although he always drew laughs, he spoke on politics, international problems, and other serious matters.

In November 1900 he spoke to members of the Nineteenth

Century Club on "The Disappearance of Literature." At the Berkeley Lyceum he argued against foreign exploitation of China. At a banquet, he touched on China again when introducing England's young Winston Churchill.

All this took great effort. As usual, Sam wrote out and memorized his speeches and then fooled his listeners into thinking he spoke off the top of his head. The pace tired him. He lost weight and coughed persistently. Toward the end of the year, he began cutting back his schedule. He claimed to have turned down seven banquet invitations in one day.

Weary as he might be, he did not run from a fight. After a cabman overcharged Katie Leary, Sam took the man to court and made such a strong case before the press that cabdrivers throughout the city revised their fees.

Sam's opposition to Chinese exploitation came to a head after the Boxer Rebellion when he criticized heavy penalties and fines demanded of China by foreign missionaries and tradesmen. When he suggested in a sarcastic article in the *North American Review* early in 1901 that Christians were breaking their own rules of conduct, Mark Twain put the entire American Board of Foreign Missions on the defensive.

His mail increased. Although some opposed his views, Sam remained unshaken. He wrote in his notebook, "Do right and you will be conspicuous."

Sam and his family spent the summer of 1901 at a log cabin beside Saranac Lake in New York. Sam went rowing, swam, took long walks in the woods, left his letters unanswered, and did not look at a newspaper. He wrote a parody of a Sherlock Holmes story that included a literary prank he expected few readers would catch. It came in a descriptive paragraph in which flowers bloomed out of season and "far in the empty sky a solitary oeasophogus slept upon motionless wing. . . ."[1]

To his surprise, soon after the story appeared in *Harper's*, hundreds of readers wrote to say an oeasophogus was not a bird. Sam was pleased to answer these fans and congratulate them on being so perceptive.

This was the first summer that Rogers, who owned a large yacht, took Sam and several others cruising. They went to New Brunswick and Nova Scotia, but the boating party was more interested in playing poker than looking at scenery. Sam's "log" of the voyage was full of exaggerations and good fun.

Sam, Livy, and the girls settled into Wave Hill, a comfortable old house at Riverdale-on-the-Hudson where he hoped for more peace. Mark Twain, however, was not allowed to rest. In one month he and Livy entertained guests for seventeen out of their twenty-one meals at home.

In October 1901 he went to New Haven, Connecticut, where he and Howells received Doctor of Letters degrees from Yale University. At the same time, Sam had joined the campaign to reform New York politics and his speeches against Tammany Hall helped elect a reform mayor.

It was at this time, as if his correspondence were not heavy enough, that he formed the Juggernaut Club and began enlisting young girls who were willing to write to him. Although he never achieved his goal of having a correspondent in every country of the world, he had great fun with the letters.

"Some day," he wrote a new member, "I may admit males, but I don't know—they are capricious & inharmonious, & their ways provoke me a good deal."

Sam would later form other girls-only clubs, perhaps trying to fill the gap left by Susy's tragic death.

In another letter campaign at this time, Sam asked several friends to write his obituary and send it to him so he could correct it before he died—"not the facts, but the verdicts." He used some of his "death notices" in an amusing article for *Harper's Weekly*.

Meanwhile, his protest grew against the "wanton war and robbing expedition"[2] waged by the United States in the Philippines. "We are as indisputedly in possession of a wide-spreading archipelago as if it were our property; we have pacified some thousands of islanders and buried them; destroyed their fields; burned their villages, and turned their widows and orphans out-of-doors."[3]

Sam eventually became so bitter over the acquisition of the Philippines by the United States that he wrote his famous War Prayer.

O Lord our God, help us to tear their soldiers to bloody shreds with our shells; help us to cover their smiling fields with the pale forms of their patriot dead; help us to drown the thunder of the guns with the wounded, writhing in pain; help us to lay waste their humble homes with a hurricane of fire; help us to wring the hearts of their unoffending widows with unavailing grief; help us to turn them out roofless with their little children to wander unfriended through wastes of their desolate land in rags & hunger & thirst, sport for the sun-flames of summer & the icy winds of winter, broken in spirit, worn with travail, imploring Thee for the refuge of the grave & denied it—for our sakes, who adore Thee, Lord, blast their hopes, blight their lives, protract their bitter pilgrimage, make heavy their steps, water their way with tears, stain the white snow with the blood of their wounded feet! We ask of one who is the Spirit of love & is the ever-faithful refuge & friend of all that are sore beset, & seek His aid with humble & contrite hearts. Grant our prayer, O Lord & Thine shall be the praise & honor & glory now & ever, Amen.[4]

Sam returned to Hannibal as a celebrity in 1902. Here he stands before the Clemens home on Hill Street.

Now approaching his sixty-seventh birthday, Sam had not expected to see Hannibal or his childhood friends again, but in the spring of 1902, the University of Missouri asked him west to accept an honorary degree.

It was a joyful journey. His old river pilot friend Horace Bixby was waiting for him at the St. Louis railroad station, and a huge crowd staged an impromptu reception at his hotel. Next, he and Bixby went to a pilots' gathering where more old comrades greeted him.

Sam spent five happy days in Hannibal. He distributed diplomas at the high school graduation. He posed for photos outside his old home on Hill Street. He toured the town and the countryside in a carriage. On Sunday he spoke at each church, claiming it was the church responsible for his early Bible training. He made the claim even in churches built long after he had left town. One evening he was so moved by a program staged in his honor by the Labinnah (Hannibal spelled backward) Club, that he ended his speech in tears.

At every stop during the train journey from Hannibal to the Columbia campus of the university, crowds gathered to cheer him. His arms overflowed with flowers. Bands played. He tried to voice his gratitude, but often he could only stand silently with a tight throat and tear-swollen eyes.

On June 4, when the graduation ceremonies began, Sam thought he had his emotions under control. He led the academic procession, distributed diplomas, and even received his own honorary doctor of law degree without a hitch. But then he turned to the crowd. Was he supposed to say something? While he hesitated, the entire audience rose and stood in silent respect before him.

Sam broke down entirely and did not recover until after the students broke into a chant, spelling out M-I-S-S-O-U-R-I with high spirit and lusty cheers. Then Sam managed a few words of thanks.

✒ CHAPTER **25**

Death in Florence

Why is it that we rejoice at a birth and grieve at a funeral? It is because we are not the person involved.

Soon after Sam returned to Riverdale, Rogers came up the Hudson in his yacht, took the Clemens family on board and sailed to York Harbor, Maine, where Sam and Livy had rented a cabin. A pleasant, productive summer began.

Howells, who had rented nearby, visited daily and sat with Sam on a big veranda to talk and look down through the pines at the York River. They often read to each other from work in progress.

This simple, carefree routine was broken one August morning when Livy woke with a racing pulse and labored breath. A doctor ordered rest. Sam, terribly frightened, hired nurses and turned away all visitors. Although Livy's pulse returned to normal, she remained weak and unable to travel until October.

Back at Riverdale, Clara took charge of the household while Livy spent several more months in bed. When she finally did get on her feet again, she had so little energy she needed solitude. Even Sam's visits had to be limited to a few minutes each day. He wrote her notes and slipped them under her bedroom door.

Sam worked on a story about Huck Finn and Tom Sawyer that jumped back and forth from their youth to a period years later when they return as adults to their hometown. This gave him a chance to describe his own emotions during his recent visit to Hannibal, but unable to end the story to his satisfaction, he put it aside unfinished.

By the spring of 1903 he had seen his family through another health crisis. Jean, never robust, had come down with pneumonia. Somehow the Clemens household kept the news from Livy. Even when Jean lay close to death, her temperature at 104 degrees, Livy knew nothing of it. The ordeal tortured Sam, but most of the burden fell on Clara. Never before had she lied to her mother, but now she invented stories to conceal her sister's illness.

Sam wrote Twichell, "Now, Joe, just see what reputation can do. All Clara's life she has told Livy the truth and now the reward comes; Clara lies to her three and a half hours every day, and Livy takes it all at par, whereas even when I tell her the truth it isn't worth much without corroboration. . . ."

Jean gradually improved. Livy remained weak. The exhausted Clara fell ill. Sam suffered from bronchitis. Then Jean came down with measles. On February 2, 1903, Sam and Livy marked their thirty-third wedding anniversary by spending five whole minutes together, three more minutes than the nurse usually allowed.

Except for letters, he wrote little. His worries even made reading difficult. He did enjoy Helen Keller's *Story of My Life,* however, and wrote the author to congratulate her.

Sam turned down almost all invitations and requests for

interviews. He declined to run for president of the United States after a group of fans backed by a newspaper editor endorsed his candidacy. When Missouri fans tried to form a Mark Twain Association, he wrote the organizers, "I hope that no society will be named for me while I am still alive, for I might at some time or other do something which would cause its members to regret having done me that honor." Until his death, he predicted, he would remain "a doubtful quantity, like the rest of our race."

They spent the summer at Quarry Farm where the quiet and the warm summer air restored health to Sam's patients. Livy eventually gained enough strength to ride out with Sam in the carriage. Greatly relieved, he was able to work again and spent many hours in his isolated office. Meanwhile, he and Livy made plans for another winter in Florence, Italy.

On October 5, 1903, they put flowers on Susy's grave and returned to Riverdale to prepare for the trip. Money would be no problem. Sam had signed an agreement with Harper and Brothers that guaranteed him a minimum of twenty-five thousand dollars a year for the next five years for whatever he wrote.

Sam, Livy, Clara, and Jean, with Katie Leary, their maid of twenty-three years, and Margaret Sherry, a trained nurse, sailed for Italy on October 24, 1903.

Villa Viviani was not available, so Sam reluctantly rented the four-hundred-year-old Villa Reale di Quarto, a palace with more than sixty rooms. It was too large, too unkept, too cold, and too dreary to please anyone. The plumbing was uncooperative, sometimes rebellious. But the family made the best of it, occupying southern rooms that offered a view of Florence.

Rain and heavy fogs dampened their spirits, but Livy, although she had bad days, continued to improve, and Sam was able to write. In a letter to Twichell dated January 7, 1904, he said he had written thirty-seven thousand words in twenty-five days, and this did not count work that "will not see print until I am dead."

In February Livy again developed a racing pulse. An injection of brandy was needed to bring it back to normal. She remained so feeble for a time that when Sam learned that Mollie Clemens, Orion's widow, had died, he kept the news from Livy.

Clara, who had resumed her voice studies, gave a concert in April that Sam declared a triumph, but Livy's health soon demanded all their attention. A relapse kept her confined in bed, and Sam, his visits again restricted, once more began slipping notes under her door.

Although they had grown used to the palace, it was impossible to keep it in repair. Sam began to look for another villa. On June 5, with Livy apparently getting better, Sam and Jean found a smaller place that seemed perfect. When they returned to the palace, Sam spent a full hour enthusiastically describing the new villa to Livy.

He finally left her room at eight P.M., but promised to return to say good night. Then he went downstairs to play the piano.

Livy could hear the music as she prepared for sleep. "He is singing a good night carol to me," she told Margaret Sherry. Livy never spoke again.

When Sam came to say good night, she was dead.

"I was surprised and troubled that she did not notice me. Then we understood & our hearts broke. . . ."[1]

Sam brought his daughters home in June, and on July 14, 1904, they buried Olivia Langdon Clemens, fifty-eight, beside Susy and little Langdon in the family plot at Elmira.

Sam went to Tyringham, Massachusetts, where friends had offered a summer cottage. He answered condolence letters and made a few entries in his notebook. Nothing more. Meanwhile, Clara, exhausted from caring for her mother, had gone into seclusion to regain her health. Jean remained frail.

In the fall of 1904, however, Jean was able to help Sam establish a new home in a house at the corner of Ninth Street and Fifth Avenue in New York. They brought furniture out of storage from Hartford and purchased an organ which they took turns playing.

Sam rarely went out. He suffered bouts with bronchitis, but managed to write almost daily. Between articles, he worked on *Eve's Diary,* little more than a tribute to Livy and an affirmation of his love for her.

He also wrote about the need for new copyright laws and attacked the czar of Russia for his repression of Jews. Both articles were printed in the *North American Review.* After the magazine said Sam's attack on the king of Belgium for atrocities in the Congo was too strong for its readers, Sam gave the article to the Congo Reform Association. The association published it in a booklet and sold it to support its work.

❦ CHAPTER 26

Albert Bigelow Paine

Wrinkles should merely indicate where smiles have been.

Low in spirits, Sam wrote little for publication. Death had made him bitter. Clara, who had taken over Livy's role as his editor and censor, insisted that much of Sam's work from this period be held back, and he agreed.

Sam's spirits brightened in the summer of 1905 after he rented a house in Dublin, New Hampshire, and he became a lively member of a literary colony there. His sociability and wit returned as he visited neighbors and took long walks with friends in the woods. Jean climbed the side of Mount Monadnock, which rose 3,165 feet just south of Dublin. Clara was well enough to join the family later in the summer.

Despite frequent bouts of rheumatism that summer, Sam wrote one hundred thousand words of social satire which he called "3,000 Years among the Microbes, by a Microbe, with Notes Added by the Same Hand 7,000 years later." After losing interest in it, he wrote various essays including "Interpreting the

Deity," a satire on those claiming to know God's intentions; "A Horse's Tale," attacking the cruelties of bullfighting; and "The Privilege of the Grave," dealing with free speech enjoyed by the dead. Almost none of this work was published.

In November 1905, when friends gathered at a New York restaurant to help him celebrate his seventieth birthday, Sam's emotions again betrayed him. He spoke of deaths and farewells, and ended in tears. Most of his friends, including Howells, Twichell, and Rogers cried with him.

In December the Society of Illustrators honored him with another banquet. When a girl dressed as Joan of Arc gave him a wreath, Sam was so choked with emotion that for several minutes he could not speak.

He returned to a more social life, attending many parties and speaking at many charity events. At a gathering of the Players Club, he met Albert Bigelow Paine, who had just finished a biography of cartoonist Thomas Nast. Although Sam was older by twenty-six years, he liked Paine, and soon agreed to let him become his biographer. Thus began a working friendship that would last the rest of Sam's life.

They went to work officially on the morning of January 9, 1906, in the house on Fifth Avenue. Paine asked the questions and a stenographer wrote down Sam's answers. Paine had hoped to keep things formal and businesslike, but Sam had different ideas. Morning after morning, he lay in bed in a silk dressing gown, puffing a pipe or cheap cigar. His long, entertaining answers often strayed far from the question. He sometimes commented on the news of the day or told amusing stories. When he did talk about his past, he often tangled the chronology so thoroughly that both Paine and the stenographer finished the session in confusion.

Sometimes Sam bent the truth to add humor or put himself in

a bad light. When chided about this, Sam said, "When I was younger, I could remember anything whether it happened or not."[1]

Sam enjoyed his captive audience so much that he began to behave like a king holding court. The servants, in fact, began referring to him as the King.

It took Paine a few weeks to realize that the interviews were producing more opinion than fact, and that Sam stuck closer to the truth and stopped showing off after the stenographer left for the day. Because their afternoon chats were more productive than the formal interviews, Paine began spending the entire day with Sam.

On fair days the two friends walked together on Fifth Avenue and often lunched at the Players Club. Sam welcomed Paine's attention, interest, and good company, and Paine filled his notebooks with Mark Twain quotations.

One morning before the regular interview began, a female fan was allowed a brief visit. Upon leaving, she kissed Sam's hand and exclaimed, "How God must love you!"

"I hope so," Sam replied, but as soon as she had left, he told Paine, "I guess she hasn't heard of our strained relations."[2]

During one of his frequent charity appearances, Sam was asked how long he would talk. "I cannot say for sure. It is my custom to keep on talking until I get the audience cowed. Sometimes it takes an hour and fifteen minutes, sometimes I can do it in an hour."

Sam grew to rely on Paine more and more, both for company and for advice. After Paine bought land in Redding, Connecticut, at a good price, Sam bought his own two hundred acres there, sight unseen. His property included a hilltop building site he would one day use.

When he returned to Dublin for the summer of 1906, Sam took Paine and the stenographer with him. The morning interviews continued on the veranda. In the afternoons, depending on the weather, the two friends either walked in the woods or sat inside by the fire. Rain or shine, they talked.

He did little writing, and even occasionally skipped the day's interview with Paine to go to New York. He took several days off to go cruising on Rogers's yacht.

After the *North American Review* paid thirty thousand dollars for advance publication of some of his reminiscences, Sam decided to build a house on the recently purchased Redding

Soon after this formal photo, Sam began wearing white suits year-round.

property. Because he did not want to see the house until it was finished and furnished, Clara took charge of everything.

Clara was certainly capable. As strong-willed as her father, she not only ran the household with a firm hand, but also found time to pursue her musical career. She took on the chores at Redding without complaint.

When he returned to New York, Sam decided to wear white suits year-round. White had been traditional with him every summer for several years, but he had changed to black when he returned to New York for the winter. The new outfit was unusual but apt. The white complemented his mustache and full mane of white hair, and the bright suit drew attention and comment in the drab New York winter. The white suit soon became a Mark Twain trademark.

In the city that fall, when Sam learned that Mrs. Rogers intended to give him a billiard table for Christmas, he insisted on having the gift at once. He moved his bed into his study and had the bedroom converted to a game room.

As soon as the table arrived, Sam began teaching Paine how to play the game. They played for hours, every afternoon and often late into the evening. Paine by now usually had both lunch and dinner with Sam and his family.

With so much time in the game room, Paine soon became a fair player, but Sam almost always won, and life was easier when he did. While Paine could accept defeat patiently, Sam could not. Even when winning, he could show brief fits of temper, but his good nature quickly returned. He would apologize if he thought it necessary and almost always suggest another game.

Rogers often dropped by, not to play but just to listen. Other visitors were usually shown directly to the game room. Sam let few people interrupt his play. He even spent his seventy-first birthday playing billiards with Paine.

Sam's biographer, Albert Bigelow Paine, soon became his main opponent at billiards.

In December, Sam spent several days in Washington, D.C., with several other authors, urging Congress to back stricter copyright laws. Paine served as personal secretary during the Washington visit. As the man in white, Sam was certainly the most easily recognized author and probably the most influential. When his turn came to speak before a joint committee of the House and the Senate, the gallery was jammed.

Sam entered old age with mixed feelings and a good deal of conflict. He was content to stay home in his game room with Paine day after day, but he was too gregarious to become a recluse.

He could be both generous and tightfisted. He paid his servants well, and did not complain about the price of food or clothing, but he made sure tradesmen didn't overcharge, and went about the house turning down gas jets in unoccupied rooms. He was always openhanded with friends. Steve Gillis, now an invalid, wrote from California saying that he finally had time to read Sam's books, but found he had no money to buy them. Sam immediately sent him the American Publishing Company's twenty-volume set of his works. He gave a small party early in 1907 for Helen Keller, now almost as famous as Mark Twain.

When Sam's bronchitis persisted that spring, his doctor had urged a trip to Bermuda. He persuaded Twichell to go with him. They stayed at the same boardinghouse and enjoyed the same walks and the same landmarks that they remembered from a trip to the islands thirty years before. And Sam did feel better when he returned to New York.

He might have stayed put, but Oxford University asked him to come to England to receive an honorary degree in its June ceremonies. As soon as he accepted, he was flooded with other invitations from British friends. It seemed that the entire country wanted to entertain him.

Because Paine could not go with him, Sam hired Robert Ashcroft, a young Englishman, as social secretary. They sailed on June 8, exactly forty years after Mark Twain began his famous voyage on the *Quaker City*.

The reception began as soon as the ship docked at Liverpool where stevedores doffed their hats to the man in the white suit. On the train to London it seemed that the country had declared a holiday. People lined the way to wave to him and cheer him. The station platform was jammed. His trip to Brown's Hotel was a festive parade.

In cap and gown, Sam received an honorary degree from Oxford in 1907.

Ashcroft was so overwhelmed by photographers, reporters, and mail, that Sam at once had to hire another secretary. The two worked long hours sorting through invitations and lecture requests. Sam wanted to say yes to everything, but it was not physically possible.

He joined eight hundred other guests at the king and queen's garden party at Windsor Castle where he reminded the king of their meeting in Homburg fifteen years earlier when the king was still Prince of Wales.

Sam received his honorary degree from Oxford on June 26,

1907, along with French sculptor Auguste Rodin, British author Rudyard Kipling, and several other accomplished people.

The ceremony provided only brief respite from his schedule of banquets and receptions. He received visitors regularly at lunch, tea, and dinner in his London hotel. Sometimes he even entertained visitors at breakfast.

Irish playwright George Bernard Shaw wrote after visiting Sam that his work would be as important to America as Voltaire's is to France. "I tell you so because I am the author of a play in which a priest says, 'Telling the truth is the funniest joke in the world,' a piece of wisdom that you helped teach me."[3]

Sam was having so much fun that he extended his visit, but finally, on July 13, he sailed for America, and London returned to normal. Never before had the city given a foreigner such a long and enthusiastic reception.

27

Stormfield

All say, "How hard it is that we have to die"—a strange complaint
from the mouths of people who have had to live.

Sam spent the rest of the summer of 1907 at Tuxedo Park, New York, where he had rented a house. Tired or perhaps depressed, he resumed dictation sessions with Paine at a slower pace than before, and when he returned to New York City in the fall, he tried to reduce his time in the game room.

Billiards, however, had become his addiction. He and Paine once more played far into the night. He resumed his walks on Fifth Avenue and, as always, enjoyed being recognized.

One of his charity events at this time included a talk at the Jewish Education Alliance's production of *The Prince and the Pauper* in the children's theater on the lower East Side. Sam, who had financed the production, assured a packed house with his appearance.

Although he slowed his pace, he could never ignore his mail entirely. He developed a stock answer for fans who sent him

Sam loved everything about Stormfield, his new home at Redding. He relaxes with pipe and newspaper in his study.

home remedies for bronchitis or rheumatism. He said he wanted to try every suggestion. "Yours is 2,653. I am looking forward to its beneficial results."

Early in 1908 Sam took a brief trip to Bermuda alone. Then, only a few weeks after his return, he went back to Bermuda with Rogers. Sam claimed the islands would restore Rogers's health, and indeed, they both returned from the vacation spry and in good spirits.

Meanwhile, thanks to Clara's attention, the new house at Redding was almost ready. Sam still had not seen it. "I don't want to see it until the cat is purring on the hearth."[1]

When he did finally move in, cat and all, on June 18, 1908, Sam fell in love with the place. The hilltop home was modeled after an Italian villa, complete with veranda, a reminder of happy days at Villa Viviani. There was ample space for everything, including the organ, the billiard table, the servants, and several guests.

The citizens of Redding gave Sam a big welcome. A parade of flower-draped carriages followed him along the three-mile route from the station, and fireworks lit the sky that evening. Sam and Paine played billiards until midnight.

Sam had long withheld "Captain Stormfield's Visit to Heaven," but the story, with one of his favorite fictional characters, had recently been printed. This helped him pick "Stormfield" as the name for his new home.

During one of the recent stays in Bermuda, Sam had organized the Angel Fish Club for young fans. As with the Juggernaut Club, the members were girls, and to Sam's delight, he could enlist new Angel Fish from his Redding neighbors. Meetings were held on the Stormfield veranda where the members often played the card game, hearts. With no grandchildren of his own, Sam tended to "adopt" Angel Fish as substitutes.

Cats took possession of Stormfield. There never were enough to suit Sam. A kitten on the billiard table was allowed to remain there to add interest to the game. Sam sometimes paid more attention to Danbury, Sinbad, or Tammany than he did his human guests.

Tragedy darkened the summer. On August 1, 1908, he learned that his sister Pamela's son, Samuel E. Moffett, Sam's closest male relative, had drowned at a New Jersey beach. Although young, Moffett had already become an editor of *Collier's Weekly*, an important national magazine. Sam had started him in journalism with some unusual advice:

Sam and some of the local Angel Fish play cards on the porch of Stormfield.

Go to the newspaper of your choice. Say you are idle and want work, that you are pining for work—longing for it, and that you ask no wages, and will support yourself. All that you ask is work. That you will do anything, sweep, fill the ink-stands, mucilage-bottles, run errands, and be generally useful. You must never ask for wages. You must wait until the offer of wages comes to you. You must work just as faithfully and just as eagerly as if you were being paid for it. Then see what happens.

Sam came back to Stormfield after the funeral, depressed and ill. He spent a few days in bed, then after he got up, he suffered dizziness and slight loss of memory. Eventually, however, these symptoms passed and he returned to his old schedule. He had made up his mind by now to end his days at Stormfield.

To his sister-in-law he wrote, "How Livy would love this place! How her very soul would steep itself thankfully in this peace, this tranquility, this deep stillness, this dreamy expanse of woodsy hill & valley. . . ."

By the end of the summer, Sam decided he no longer wanted to work with a stenographer. Paine, whose house was close to Stormfield, would continue to visit and take notes, but the daily interviews would stop. This gave Sam more time to read, chat with guests, and play billiards. He had breakfast when he wished, usually in bed, and he often stayed in bed to smoke and read or write most of the morning. In his notebooks, he made terse observations on current events, or jotted down a story plot, or the outline for an essay. He took very few of these ideas to completion. But he remained a faithful correspondent with his friends.

On Sunday afternoons he walked or rode out in his carriage with a friend. As always, he liked to be seen and recognized. Sam also loved to show off his new home with parties and receptions. Helen Keller came for the weekend. Laura Hawkins, the model for Becky Thatcher, now in her seventies, visited with her granddaughter. Sam encouraged friends to bring their children. He steadily enlisted more Angel Fish in the club.

Cartons of books arrived after he closed his New York home. They inspired him to establish a public library at Redding. He found a vacant chapel not far from home that could be used as a temporary library and organized a committee to plan a permanent building. One man donated a building site, others contributed money, and construction of the Mark Twain Library soon began.

On November 30, 1908, Sam marked his seventy-third

birthday in his billiard room by overseeing the installation of a marble mantel given him by the Hawaiian Promotion Committee. He passed the rest of the day admiring the gift and playing billiards with Paine.

Despite the pleasures of Stormfield, Sam had frequent bouts of pessimism. He predicted that democracy would fail in America because of "vast power and wealth, which breed commercial and political corruptions, and incite public favorites to dangerous ambitions."[2]

As for world peace, he told Paine:

Within the last generation, each Christian power has turned the bulk of its attention to finding out newer and still newer and more and more effective ways of killing Christians, and, incidentally, a pagan now and then; and the surest way to get rich quickly in Christ's earthly kingdom is to invent a kind of gun that can kill more Christians at one shot than any other existing kind. . . .

When a friend threatened to give Sam a baby elephant for Christmas, he did not realize it was a hoax. His worry mounted until Christmas Day when a two-foot-high, stuffed elephant was at last delivered to Stormfield. Sam's delight was exceeded by his immense relief.

In the spring of 1909 Clara, who had been traveling on concert tours, began spending more time at home. Jean, whose health had improved, resumed some secretarial duties for her father. She also took over an old barn to house her many pets. Rescuing stray animals had become her chief interest.

In April Sam went to Norfolk, Virginia, to speak in honor of Henry Rogers at the opening of the Virginia Railway, one of Rogers's many financial ventures. Sam described how the financier had quietly helped many friends, including himself, through difficulties, but it was the last time Sam saw his friend alive. Little more than a month later, Sam went sadly to New York to be a pallbearer at Rogers's funeral.

Meanwhile, Sam was gratified by the news that Congress at last had adopted new copyright laws, not perfect, but a move in the right direction.

In June he started for Baltimore, Maryland, to speak at the high school graduation of one of his young, letter-writing friends. On the way, he suffered his first angina pains. Although he was able to give his talk and get home safely, the trouble came back again and again.

Paine left his nearby family and moved into Stormfield in order to watch over Sam day and night. Sam tried not to complain. Even when he was uncomfortable, he went to the billiard room. Often, after a few minutes, the pain eased enough for him to enjoy a game or two. Playing took his mind off the problem. He also found that a glass of warm water gave him relief.

His doctor urged him to smoke less and take only moderate exercise, but Sam's heart was already under such stress that even a brief walk exhausted him. He often had to stop to catch his breath.

He was well enough, however, to enjoy the excitement brewing at Stormfield. Clara had met the pianist Ossip Gabrilowitsch on concert tours. He became a frequent visitor, and it was obvious that he and Clara were in love. In September, with baritone David Bisham, Clara and Gabrilowitsch staged a benefit concert for the library building fund. Soon after, they announced their engagement, saying they wanted to be married before sailing to Europe on another extended concert tour.

Joe Twichell performed the ceremony at Stormfield on October 6, 1909. Jean was Clara's bridesmaid. Jervis Langdon,

Charles Langdon's son and Clara's cousin, was best man. And Sam gave the bride away.

His writing turned even more satirical. He took the role of an immortal visitor to the planet in order to write cutting reports on what he observed. He told Paine the work would never be published, but it, along with earlier satirical works, would one day appear in *Letters from the Earth*.

Cold weather kept him inside. He reread favorite books, including *The Diary of Samuel Pepys,* Thomas Carlyle's *French Revolution,* and Richard Henry Dana, Jr.'s *Two Years Before the Mast.* He kept a volume of Kipling's poems on his bed table within easy reach.

In November Sam and Paine sailed for Bermuda, arriving in time to celebrate his seventy-fourth birthday with a few friends in his hotel. Sam read from *The Adventures of Tom Sawyer,* and later, one of the Angel Fish cut his birthday cake. The warm climate helped. His pains diminished, and some of his energy returned. He might have done well to stay longer, but he wanted to spend Christmas with Jean.

She met them at the dock on December 20, a cold, blustery day. Paine was concerned for her, but she seemed well and was excited about Christmas. Back at Stormfield she went to work at once, trimming the tree and wrapping presents.

Sam, who had stayed in New York briefly to visit friends, arrived at Stormfield on December 23, in time to have dinner with Jean. She was tired with a slight cold, but remained in high spirits. When Sam bade her good night, he had no hint it was their last farewell. Jean died alone early in the morning, either during or soon after an epileptic seizure.

No god could comfort him. No logic, no reason, no justice could be found. At seventy-four, he had lost his twenty-nine-year-old daughter, his youngest child. Sam tried to be stoic, and

Reading in bed became a favorite pastime. This is one of many photos taken by Albert Bigelow Paine.

to find solace he picked up his pen and wrote objectively and with painstaking detail all the events of that awful day from the moment Jean's body was found until she was finally carried from the house. "I am setting it down, everything. It is a relief to me to write it. It furnishes me an excuse for thinking."[3] He described the half-decorated Christmas tree, the scatter of wrapping paper, even the large globe of the world that Jean had planned to give him. He wrote it all down. All of it.

He cabled Clara and her husband to tell them of the tragedy and urge them not to interrupt their European tour. Jervis

Langdon came from Elmira to help make arrangements. Paine and his family stayed in Stormfield to keep Sam company.

Sam was too ill, too brokenhearted to make the trip to Elmira where Jean was buried. He stayed home and continued writing about Jean's death. When he finished, he put down his pen and told Paine he would never write again.

He had forgotten, however, that there would soon be scores of condolence letters that must be answered.

In the evenings, instead of billiards, Sam preferred to listen to Paine play the organ. Traditional Highland tunes such as "Bonnie Doon" and "The Campbells Are Coming" were among his favorites.

He sailed alone for Bermuda on January 5, 1910, to stay with his friends the Allens, whose daughter, Helen, had become a favorite Angel Fish. He met Woodrow Wilson, then vacationing from his job as president of Princeton University. They had a long talk. Wilson later would become twenty-eighth president of the United States.

The affectionate attention of the Allens and other island friends restored Sam's spirits. The warm climate somewhat restored his health. The chest pains became milder and less frequent. By the end of March, however, the pains intensified once more. Mrs. Allen summoned Paine, who sailed for Bermuda at once.

He found Sam in good spirits, but thinner and in need of morphine injections whenever the pains struck. It seemed for a time that Sam would be too weak for an ocean voyage, but he rallied and sailed with Paine in mid-April.

When the ship entered cold weather, Sam began to have so much trouble breathing that Paine had to hold him up in bed in a half-sitting position. Later, with pillows supporting Sam, Paine was able to read to him. Morphine made Sam drowsy, but the effort to breathe kept him awake.

He reached New York exhausted and had to be carried from the ship. He entered Stormfield on his feet, however, and insisted on greeting friends and servants in his usual courtly manner. Then he allowed himself to be carried upstairs and put to bed.

The end would come soon. Clara and Ossip, who had already been summoned from Europe, arrived at Stormfield on April 17. That day Clara talked hopefully with Sam about his summer plans. He was lucid, but the next day, breathing heavily, his mind began to wander.

He managed to read a few lines from one of his favorite books, but conversation was difficult. Clara sang to him, but when she read him some of the messages from friends and fans, Sam was unresponsive.

On Wednesday night, April 20, 1910, Halley's comet, which lit the sky when Sam was born, glowed bright enough to be seen once again with the naked eye. Sam seemed better the next morning, and he read a little and talked to Paine. Then his voice failed. With a shaking hand, he had to write his request for a drink of water and his eyeglasses.

At noon, while holding Clara's hand, he was able to say good-bye in a weak voice. Then he fell into his final sleep. He stopped breathing at about 6:30 P.M., April 21, 1910.

Although the entire world mourned, the funeral in New York's Brick Presbyterian Church was brief and simple. Twichell stood beside his old friend and, with his voice breaking in grief, recited a poem. Thousands filed through the church for a last view of Mark Twain. He lay among flowers, splendid in his white suit.

Later at Elmira, he was buried beside those he loved.

NOTES

Chapter One
1. Quoted by Margaret Sanborn in *Mark Twain, The Bachelor Years.*

Chapter Four
1. *Life on the Mississippi* by Mark Twain.
2. *Ibid.*

Chapter Six
1. *Roughing It* by Mark Twain.

Chapter Seven
1. Quoted from a newspaper clipping by the editors of *Mark Twain's Letters, Vol. 1, 1853–1866.*

Chapter Eight
1. From a newspaper clipping quoted by Albert Bigelow Paine.
2. Quoted by Paine.
3. *The Autobiography of Mark Twain.*
4. *Ibid.*

Chapter Nine
1. *Roughing It* by Mark Twain.
2. Quoted by the editors of *Mark Twain's Letters, Vol. 1, 1853–1866.*
3. *Ibid.*
4. Quote by Paine from one of Mark Twain's notebooks.

Chapter Ten
1. Quotes taken from the original poster as reproduced in *Mark Twain's San Francisco.*
2. Quoted by the editors of *Mark Twain's Letters, Vol. 2, 1867–1868.*
3. Quoted from the *Alta California* by the editors of *Mark Twain's Letters, Vol. 2, 1867–1868.*

Chapter Eleven
1. Quoted from the *Cleveland Plain Dealer* by the editors of *Mark Twain's Letters, Vol. 2, 1867–1868.*
2. Quoted by Paine from Mark Twain's notes.
3. Quoted by the editors of *Mark Twain's Letters, Vol. 2, 1867–1868.*
4. *Ibid.*

Chapter Twelve
1. Quoted by Paine.
2. *Ibid.*

Chapter Thirteen
1. Quoted by Paine.
2. Quoted by Paine from Mark Twain's recollection of the conversation.

Chapter Fifteen
1. Quoted by Paine.

Chapter Sixteen
1. Quoted by Paine.
2. *Ibid.*

Chapter Seventeen
1. Quoted by Paine.
2. Quoted by Paine from one of Mark Twain's notebooks.

Chapter Eighteen
1. Quoted by Paine from one of Mark Twain's notebooks.
2. Quoted by Paine.
3. *Ibid.*

Chapter Nineteen
1. Quoted by Paine.
2. Quoted from one of Mark Twain's notebooks.
3. Quoted by Paine from a Mark Twain memorandum.
4. Quoted from Susy Clemens's journal.

Chapter Twenty
1. Quoted by Paine from a Mark Twain memorandum.
2. Quoted by Paine.

Chapter Twenty-one
1. Quoted by Paine.
2. Quoted by Paine from one of Mark Twain's notebooks.
3. Quoted by Paine from Mark Twain's recollection of the conversation.

Chapter Twenty-two
1. Quoted by Paine from Olivia Clemens's correspondence.
2. From *Following the Equator* by Mark Twain.
3. From introductory remarks to an Australian audience.

Chapter Twenty-three
1. Quoted by Paine from reporter's interview.
2. Quoted by Paine.
3. *Ibid.*
4. *Ibid.*
5. *Ibid.*
6. *Ibid.*

Chapter Twenty-four
1. From "The Double Barreled Detective Story" by Mark Twain.
2. Quoted by Paine.
3. *Ibid.*
4. From "The War Prayer" by Mark Twain.

Chapter Twenty-five
1. In a letter to William Dean Howells by Mark Twain.

Chapter Twenty-six
1. Quoted by Paine.
2. *Ibid.*
3. *Ibid.*

Chapter Twenty-seven
1. Quoted by Paine.
2. *Ibid.*
3. *Ibid.*

BOOKS BY MARK TWAIN

The Celebrated Jumping Frog of Calaveras County and Other Sketches, 1867
The Innocents Abroad, 1869
Roughing It, 1872
The Gilded Age, with Charles Dudley Warner, 1874
Sketches, New and Old, 1875
The Adventures of Tom Sawyer, 1876
A Tramp Abroad, 1880
The Prince and the Pauper, 1882
The Stolen White Elephant, 1882
Life on the Mississippi, 1883
Adventures of Huckleberry Finn, 1885
A Connecticut Yankee in King Arthur's Court, 1889
An American Claimant, 1892
The Tragedy of Pudd'nhead Wilson, 1894
The Personal Recollections of Joan of Arc, 1896
Tom Sawyer Abroad; Tom Sawyer, Detective; and Other Stories, 1896
Following the Equator, 1897
The Man That Corrupted Hadleyburg, 1900
What Is Man?, 1906
The Mysterious Stranger, posthumously, 1916

SELECT BIBLIOGRAPHY

Allen, Jerry. *The Adventures of Mark Twain*. Boston: Little, Brown and Company, 1954.

Kaplan, Justin. *Mr. Clemens and Mark Twain: A Biography*. New York: Simon and Schuster, 1966.

Paine, Albert Bigelow. *Mark Twain, A Biography*. 3 vols. New York: Harper & Brothers, 1912.

Sanborn, Margaret. *Mark Twain, The Bachelor Years*. New York: Doubleday Dell Publishing Group, 1990.

Steinbrink, Jeffrey. *Getting to Be Mark Twain*. Berkeley: University of California Press, 1991.

Tuckey, John S. *The Devil's Race-Track, Mark Twain's Great Dark Writings*. Berkeley: University of California Press, 1980.

Twain, Mark. *The Autobiography of Mark Twain*. Edited by Charles Neider. New York: Harper & Row, 1959.

——. *The Complete Essays of Mark Twain*. Edited by Charles Neider. Garden City, N.Y.: Doubleday & Company, 1963.

——. *The Complete Short Stories of Mark Twain*. Edited by Charles Neider. Garden City, N.Y.: Doubleday & Company, 1957.

——. *The Forgotten Writings of Mark Twain*. Edited by Henry Duskis. New York: Philosophical Library, 1963.

——. *Letters from the Earth*. Edited by Bernard DeVoto. New York: Harper & Row, 1962.

——. *Mark Twain in Eruption*. Edited by Bernard DeVoto. New York and London: Harper, 1922.

————. *Mark Twain's America.* Edited by Bernard DeVoto. Boston: Houghton Mifflin Co., 1932.

————. *Mark Twain's Autobiography.* 2 vols. Edited by Albert Bigelow Paine. New York: Harper & Brothers, 1924.

————. *Mark Twain's Letters.* Edited by Albert Bigelow Paine. New York: Harper, 1917.

————. *Mark Twain's Letters: Vol. 1. 1853–1866.* Edited by Edgar Marquess Branch, Michael B. Frank, and Kenneth M. Sanderson. Berkeley: University of California Press, 1988.

————. *Mark Twain's Letters: Vol. 2. 1867–1868.* Edited by Harriet Elinor Smith and Richard Bucci. Berkeley: University of California Press, 1990.

————. *Mark Twain's Letters: Vol. 3. 1869.* Edited by Victor Fischer and Michael B. Frank. Berkeley: University of California Press, 1992.

————. *Mark Twain's Notebooks & Journals, Vol. 1.* Edited by Frederick Anderson, Michael B. Frank, and Kenneth M. Sanderson. Berkeley: University of California Press, 1975.

————. *Mark Twain's Notebooks & Journals, Vol. 2.* Edited by Frederick Anderson, Lin Salamo, and Bernard L. Stein. Berkeley: University of California Press, 1975.

————. *Mark Twain's Notebooks & Journals, Vol. 3.* Edited by Robert Pack Browning, Michael B. Frank, and Lin Salamo. Berkeley: University of California Press, 1979.

————. *Mark Twain's San Francisco.* Edited by Bernard Taper. New York: McGraw-Hill, 1963.

Index

Page numbers in italics refer to illustrations.